The Rottentrolls II
...With a Vengeance (sort of)

Written by Graham Marks
Illustrations by Gordon Firth

Based on the TV series by Tim Firth

MADCAP

Also available from Madcap Books

Roger and the Rottentrolls I in Reigning Sheep
and Trolls
Jimjam YaHA! The Secret World of the
Rottentrolls

First published in Great Britain in 1998 by
Madcap Books, André Deutsch Ltd
76 Dean Street, London W1V 5HA
www.vci.co.uk

André Deutsch Ltd is a VCI plc company

Based on the scripts of the TV series, Roger and the Rottentrolls,
written by Tim Firth and produced by The Children's Company

A catalogue record for this book is available from the
British Library

ISBN 0 233 99253 7

Printed in Great Britain

PROLOGUE

In case you've never heard of Roger, or have any idea what a Rottentroll is, and have got this book because it's been bought by some well-meaning old auntie (who just happens to have made the most incredible choice, by the way), here's a few tips and bits of useful info.

1 – Don't panic, there's no actual information in this book, nothing you'll be tested on later.

2 – Roger Becket may only be $10^3/4$ but he's still our hero. He lives with his Mum and Stepdad and discovered Troller's Ghyll while out cycling one day.

3 – Troller's Ghyll is a hidden valley on the endless moor, and it's where the Rottentrolls live.

4 – Rottentrolls are small, three-foot high Norwegian trolls whose ancestors, many, many years ago, were picked up in a snow cloud by mistake by the great magician Merlin. As they fell out of the sky, onto what was supposed to be a new royal ski resort, they heard Merlin say, 'Those rotten trolls have messed it all up!' And from that day they've known their true name to be Rottentrolls.

5 – Rottentrolls are, by and large, mad.

6 – The stupidest one is called Yockenthwaite. He makes cottage cheese look intelligent.

7 – The cleverest one is called Penyghent. She's a girl, but that's not her fault.

8 – It's her Dad's fault, and he's called Aysgarth; he's the most important of the Rottentrolls – which doesn't mean much, believe me.

9 – Rottentrolls like to eat garlic pasties. Actually they *have* to eat garlic pasties because that's all that Kettlewell, the dangerous chef, can cook. Her daughter is called Little Strid. There is, as far as I can work out, no Big Strid.

10 – Trucklecrag isn't a dangerous magician, he's a disappointing one.

11 – Sigsworthy Crags is mad as a stuck pig.

12 – The Nab Twins are teenagers and will grow out of it, eventually.

13 (or 12a if you're superstitious) – Roger is King of the Rottentrolls because Yockenthwaite heard him shout 'Roger was 'ere!'...and that's the ancient name the Rottentrolls found carved in a stone in the Great Cave.

14 – Rottentrolls have never heard of graffiti.

15 – Commander Harris isn't a Rottentroll. He's a sheep. He's also a master of the ancient martial art of Jimjam YaHa ('Combat without contact!') which he picked up in the jungle while he was a mascot with the Army. He is ALSO leader of the Troller's Ghyll SAS (Silently Armed Sheep).

16 – The Barguest is a monster, with enormous red eyes as large as dinner plates. It lives in the old abandoned lead mines and comes out when the moon is full. It likes to eat Rottentrolls.

17 – Now read on. It'll all make sense, honest...

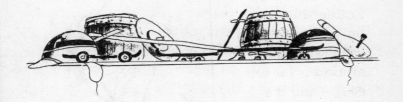

PART 1 (The Civil War)

You might think being a King was a pretty fantastic job. You know, wearing a crown, bossing people about, everyone doing exactly what you told them to...that kind of thing. This might be the case if you were King Henry VIII (who also got to chop the wife's head off if he got fed up with her), or King Zog of Albania (I am *not* making this up, honest), but if you were King of the Rottentrolls, like Roger Becket of Hugh Gaitskell Crescent, Cowgill (and I'm not making that up either), life would be a little different.

For starters, your crown isn't up to much. And then, Rottentrolls are only three feet tall – so bossing them around is far too easy – and it's amazing how much trouble you can cause when people who aren't much brighter than the chairs they sit in do *exactly* what you tell them to.

Anyway, enough of history. Today King Roger was out playing hide-and-seek with Yockenthwaite, which was practically an impossibility on a moor that was 28 square miles of endless heather.

'All right!' yelled Roger, from where he was lying down. 'I give up!'

'Yo-o!' shouted a tiny figure, bobbing up 28 miles away. 'I win!'

'Fine...end of game,' said Roger, getting up and reaching for the bulging plastic bag on the ground next to him, 'I've got to go to the tip.'

'What are you getting rid of?' asked

Penyghent, who happened to be passing by.
'These,' explained Roger, taking something out
of the bag, 'loads of old comics from under me
bed.'

'*The Power Surfers?*' asked Great Nab, looking
over Roger's shoulder.

'Yeah, I've grown out of all that now...all that
"superheroes defending the earth" stuff,' nodded Roger, taking the comic back. 'I'm gonna
throw them in the recycling thing outside Asda.'

Slinging the bag over his shoulder, Roger
walked off, not realising a comic had come
flying out behind him. The Nab Twins locked
onto it like a radar onto a flying saucer, looked
at each other and then raced off after it. Y'see,
the thing was, King Roger might've grown out
of reading comics...he might've grown out of
cartoons about superhuman superheroes
defending the earth and all that stuff...but,
tragically, the Rottentrolls hadn't...

'We are the Power Surfers!'
came a mighty superheroic-
type battle cry from the
Nab Twins, Askrigg and
Yockenthwaite. They
were all dressed up in
home-made capes
and masks and

were holding skateboardy type things and what were supposed to be light sabres.

Then they all took off down a slope on their skateboards, shouting:

'Go-go Power Surfers!'

Except for Yockenthwaite, who muttered:

'Go! Oh 'eck, me wheel's come off – hold on!'

'Right, what shall we do today?' said Askrigg. 'Yeah! We'll save the world from the forces of Princess Zeebo and her evil Doom Warriors!'

'I know,' said Yockenthwaite, 'why don't us lot invite them over one evening and sit round a table and have a good chat...'

'*Chat?*' interrupted Great Nab.

'...about problems, and have...'

'*Chat?*' echoed Small Nab.

'...a nice cup of tea...'

'*CHAT?*' frowned Askrigg.

'...and cake.'

'Power Surfers don't 'chat', you twirp!' said Great Nab.

'No,' said Small Nab, 'we do, like, incredibly dangerous things like...like...'

'Like going into the disused lead mines where the Barguest lives!' grinned Askrigg.

And so, not long after that...

'What are y'doing? Come back!' pleaded Yockenthwaite, standing outside the disused lead mines where the Barguest lived. 'We can't go in there – what if the Barguest comes out with his massive teeth and eyes as big as dinner plates, eh?'

'Are you scared, Power Surfer Number 4?' asked Great Nab.

'Well...well...well,' stammered Yockenthwaite, 'it's not a case of being *scared*...'

'He's scared,' said Small Nab.

'There's no such thing as a Scared Power Surfer, man,' sneered Great Nab.

'Yeah...right, bro,' agreed Small Nab, 'we're the Non-scared Power Surfers – and you're not one of us, so get lost!'

Non-scared Power Surfers Numbers 1, 2 and 3 (otherwise known as the Nab Twins and Askrigg) scooted off, leaving ex-Power Surfer Number 4 to wander back to his cave on his own...which is where Roger found him, sobbing his little Rottentroll heart out.

'What's the matter?' he asked.

'Nothing! Everything's fine!' said Yocken-thwaite, trying to look like he was as happy as a pig in, well, what pigs like to be happy in. 'I'm just doing a bit of cleaning, polishing and, y'know, baking...'

'You sure?' enquired Roger.

'*NO-OOOOOOOOOOOOOO!!!*' bawled Yockenthwaite.

It took quite some time, and a lot of handker-chiefs (funny word that, handkerchief, if you think about it...) but Roger eventually managed to piece together the story about the comic, and the Power Surfers (1,2,3 and 4), and the disused lead mines, and the Barguest and finally the Non-scared Power Surfers (just 1,2 and 3).

'...and they threw me out the gang, King Roger,' sniffed Yockenthwaite, "cos I wouldn't go with them.'

'I think you did a *brilliant* thing, Yockenthwaite,' said Roger. 'You knew it was dangerous to go into the Barguest's cave, but you didn't go just because everyone else wanted to go.'

'Yeah, yeah, yeah,' sulked Yockenthwaite, chucking a pot across the room. 'So I've been 'good'...but that doesn't help me now, does it? I'm still here on me own, aren't I? Still got no gang.'

'Look, Yockenthwaite,' said Roger, 'if you ever find you're not in someone else's gang, the best thing to do is...'

'Go into a complete retreat from humanity,' Yockenthwaite huffed, 'and live with your Mum for the rest of your life in a dark room.'

'No – start a gang of your own...'

I don't think Roger had it in mind to *actually* join Yockenthwaite's new gang, but as only one other person would (Penyghent, who only joined out of sympathy), Roger sort of had to – two-people gangs being a bit of a stupid idea – but not half as stupid as...

'What are we called?' sighed Roger, standing in a large wooden barrel wearing deedly-boppers, a cape and holding a cardboard tube 'sword' and a dustbin lid shield.

'We're the, er...the er...Barrel Rangers!' said a muffled voice from inside another barrel.

'This is just *stupid!*' agreed a second muffled voice from inside a third barrel.

'Right...' sighed Roger again, looking at the two empty barrels next to him (Penyghent and Yockenthwaite were actually in theirs, but being so short you couldn't see them.)

'We're the Barrel Rangers and we're off to save the world!' said Yockenthwaite.

'We can't,' said Penyghent, 'we're in *barrels*...'

'No we're not – we're in super erm…Wood-o-Tronic defence shields!'

'WE'RE IN *BARRELS*, YOCKENTHWAITE,' screamed Penyghent, chucking her 'sword' out in disgust, 'AND THIS IS POINTLESS AND *COMPLETELY* RIDICULOUS!'

'What was that that went over my head?' said Yockenthwaite.

'My sword…'

'Get that back, Barrel Ranger One – you're gonna need that to save the world!' ordered Yockenthwaite. 'Go-go Barrel Rangers!'

Yockenthwaite tried to 'Go-go!' But the moment he went-went, his barrel fell over with a dull thud.

'Can I make a suggestion here?' asked Roger.

'I've hit me head...' groaned Yockenthwaite.

'I think we should become the Not-Barrel Rangers...'

'No!' said Yockenthwaite, struggling out onto the heather. 'The 'Power Surfers' have got their surfboards, and if we don't have our barrels we'll just be 'Rangers'... just ... just people who go round parks saying things like, "How would you like it if we did that in *your* garden!"'

'Oh, all right...' shrugged Roger.

This, as Roger would soon find out, was not going to be one of the most sensible things a King could agree to do. Not only was getting anywhere in a barrel very difficult, but when you got there the reaction was...

'A-Hahahahaha! Check out the loser gang, man!' cackled Great Nab.

'Yeah – totally, like, *spurious!*' said Small Nab.

'Who are you calling a 'loser'?' yelled Yockenthwaite, as his barrel fell over, again.

'YOU!!' shouted Askrigg and the Nab Twins.

'WE'RE THE BEST GANG, WE ARE!' came Yockenthwaite's reply. 'THE BARREL RANGERS ARE BETTER THAN THE POWER SURFERS, ANY DAY!'

'What use are barrels if you've got to fight Queen Zeebo and her evil Doom Warriors?' taunted Small Nab.

'So – what use are *surfboards* if you've got to, er...' Yockenthwaite stopped and thought for a moment, '...store lots of grit!'

'BARREL BERKS!!'

'STUPID SURFERS!!'

'Let's not get into a civil war here,' said Roger, waving his arms like a boxing referee.

'What's that?' asked Penyghent.

'It's when people from the same country fight each other,' explained Roger.

Everyone stopped what they were doing and pondered on this idea, and then...continued the civil war.

'He's not one of us,' shouted Small Nab, pointing at Yockenthwaite, 'he's a Rubbish Ranger!'

'Well you're a Power Prawn!' retaliated Yockenthwaite.

'Oh, for crying out loud...' sighed Roger.

The Civil War...well, let's be honest and up front about this, it was more of a rude, Un-civil War really...went on for quite a while...

'Big nose!'
 'Stupid bobble-hat head!'

...until King Roger and Penyghent got totally bored with it all and fell asleep. Which was a shame, because it meant neither the Barrel Ranger (there being only one of them left awake) or the Power Surfers noticed, as it got dark, that the moon which appeared in the sky was big and round and sort of, how can I put it...*full*. Which, around these parts, can only mean one thing...

'*RA-ARRRRRR!!!*'
 'Oh no!' said Penyghent, waking with a start and looking up at the night sky, and then spotting the piercing beams of two very red eyes on the nearby rocks. 'It's a full moon – it's the *Barguest* and it's coming down the valley!'
 'Quick!' said Roger, 'into that cave over there!'
 'He'll see us, man,' panted Great Nab as they hurtled into a nearby cave.
 'We'll get eaten!' Yockenthwaite began to sob. 'I *knew* I was never going to reach an old age!'
 'Block the entrance!' said Roger, 'Get some planks or wood or...'

'There's no wood in the cave, King Roger,' said Askrigg.

'There is,' said Penyghent, pointing to a Barrel Rangers barrel, 'if we break up our Barrel Ranger's special Wood-o-Tronic defence shields!'

'But then we'll just be Rangers...' wailed Yockenthwaite, 'just people who go round parks saying...'

'Shut it,' scowled Roger, smashing up a barrel.

Seconds later the three Wood-o-Tronic defences

had been turned into a common or garden wooden fence and stuck across the entrance to the cave. Seconds after that, the five Rottentrolls and their King saw shafts of red light coming through the gaps, and heard a ghastly snuffling sound...

'I SMELL ROTTENTROLLS...SNUFFLE... SMELL...I...HMMM. I DON'T REMEMBER THIS CAVE BEING BOARDED UP!'

'He smelt us!' whimpered Yockenthwaite. 'Why didn't I have a bath this spring...'

'Poke him through the crack!' suggested Great Nab.

'We don't have a pokey thing to poke with,' said Small Nab.

'The skateboards!' said Penyghent. 'Break one in half!'

'Good thinking,' panted Roger, snapping one across his knee and jabbing the sharp end through a gap in the barricade. 'Take that!'

'YOW-OOOOOOW!!!'

'Y'got him on the nose, King Roger!' Penyghent jumped up and down with excitement. 'The lights are going away – we're saved!'

'He's going back down the valley!' Great Nab said, looking though the gap. 'He's gone – he's really gone!'

'What are we going back to do now?' asked Penyghent, once all the back-slapping and high-fiving had finished. 'Look at all this mess...'

'D'you want me to try and put it all back together again?' asked Roger, picking up bits of Barrel Ranger Wood-o-Tronic defence shield and Power Surfer skateboard.

'Well...' said Great Nab, 'maybe not...'

'Yeah,' agreed Small Nab, 'once you've, like, fought on the same side *against* something, it seems a bit daft to go back to fighting a Civil War, dun't it?'

'Perhaps you could take all this stuff down to the tip, next time you go,' suggested Penyghent, 'along with that comic we're not going to need any more.'

'S'pose I could,' Roger nodded.

And that's exactly what he did. So, once again, peace and what Rottentrolls thought of as normality returned to the mad-shaped rocks and bilberry bushes of Troller's Ghyll. Until, that is, the day a *My Little Pony* comic blew in...but quite frankly I haven't got the heart to describe what happened that time.

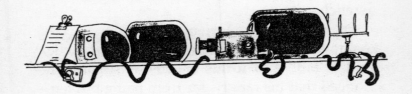

PART 2 (The Great Television Franchise)

It's amazing how one thing leads to another, isn't it? You've seen your Dad: one minute he's 'just going to clean the ashtrays in the car...' and the next he's got the engine apart on the kitchen table and your Mum's gone ballistic. Well, that's what it was like in *my* house.

Anyway, one day Commander Harris was adjusting the radar dish on top of his command hut. This was because a strong wind had moved it and, instead of picking up sheep movements in Northern Europe, it was picking up Religious Movements in Central America. But, sheep being a bit lacking in the finger department, instead of manoeuvring it delicately back into position, he knocked it off its mast so the thing was hanging by a wire, and as I say, one thing led to another.

'Oh damn, corruption and hell for Sir Harry!' muttered the Commander, abseiling back down off the roof and going to get a sprocket wrench.

As he turned to leave the hut he heard a click and a 'bip!' and to his enormous surprise he noticed that his radar – far from being broken – was actually picking something up. Not sheep movements. Not *anyone's* movements. It was picking up television! Now you might not think that was so extraordinary, but the Rottentrolls had never seen any television before. So when King Roger came to the valley the next day and yelled out...

'Morning! Anyone fancy playing Rat-Up-A - Drainpipe?'

...he thought it a bit odd that no one answered. And when he came back in full footy gear and said...

'I'm thinking of playing three-and-in. Anyone up for it?'

...he was amazed at the lack of response. Then he spotted the flickering light coming from the Commander's hut and went to investigate. Inside he found all the Rottentrolls packed together like baked beans in a can, sitting stock still, mouths open, eyes dead, staring at a TV screen.

'I've built a rollercoaster ride down the valley, with 360 degree loops and a 60 foot vertical drop!' he said. 'Anyone want a go?'

'Really?' said Aysgarth, without looking round.

'Course I haven't!' scowled Roger, 'I was just trying to get you lot away from that TV set!'

Realising that this fascination with television was because they'd never come across it before, Roger closed the door and went home. He'd been through this kind of thing himself...like when he'd first got his Gameboy. He'd played with it so much that his parents had taken him to the doctor because they'd thought he'd lost the power of speech. So he decided to give the Rottentrolls a day and come back when they'd got over the attraction of adverts and game shows and soap operas.

'Morning!' Roger called out brightly the next day, on his arrival in the valley. 'Mmm, no one's in their cave – that's a good sign, they must've got up early...'

No they hadn't. They'd actually stayed up all night watching telly and were, by now, totally brain-dead...although with someone like Yockenthwaite this was pretty hard to spot.

'Right!' said Roger, bursting into the Command Hut. 'Everyone in the Great Cave. NOW!'

Eventually they were all gathered round the table, looking bleary-eyed and slightly twitchy...the way you do when you've watched 24 hours of non-stop drivel.

'It's *completely* ridiculous,' Roger thumped the table, 'to stay up all night watching TV!'

'You're *absolutely* right,' agreed Aysgarth, thumping the table as well.

'I suggest everyone now goes back to their own cave and has a few hours sleep,' said Roger very firmly.

'Very good idea, King Roger,' nodded Aysgarth.

'Then, if you all get up about half past mid-day, or something...' Roger went on.

'It'll be time for *Name That Vegetable!!*' yelled Great Nab.

'NO!' yelled Roger.

'WA-*HEY!*' yelled the Rottentrolls.

But he was too late. All the Rottentrolls piled out of the Great Cave, high-tailed it back to Commander Harris's and settled down in front of the box again. Roger was having none of this and, storming off after them, he went right up to the TV and switched it off. Very Kingly behaviour.

'Everyone STOP crying!' said King Roger, two seconds after having turned the TV off. 'We're still going to have fun with television...only we're all going to do something a bit more *creative* than just sitting 'watching' it!'

'Like what, man?' asked Great Nab.

'Like *making* it!' beamed Roger, holding up a cine camera he'd borrowed from his step-dad. 'I hereby announce the opening of RTV!'

'Our TV?' frowned Yockenthwaite. 'I thought it was Commander Harris's...'

'No, 'RTV' – Rottentroll Television, our own TV station!' said Roger.

'Excellent idea!' said Aysgarth. 'Let's get cracking on a documentary. I think a programme about the effects of too much rain on the colour of moss would be right fascinating!'

'Woah, hold on a minute, man,' Great Nab said, standing up. 'What about game shows?'

'No, no!' Aysgarth shook his head, 'television is here to educate us. It should be, you know, things like debates on history and art.'

'Boring!' said Small Nab, 'TV should be fun – it should be about stupid video clips and people getting icky gunge dropped on them!'

'Shush, the lot of you!' Roger thumped the table again. 'OK, so there's two opinions on what RTV should be like, so you can each make a sample and then *I'll* decide which is best. I think it's called awarding a franchise.'

Under the banner of *Sensible Television*, Asygarth, Penyghent, Kettlewell and Trucklecrag sat down in a cave to plan some great educational programmes.

Under the sign *Yo-o Radical Television*, on the other hand, the Nab Twins, Yockenthwaite and Askrigg didn't bother with all that boring planning business and began programme-making. Well, started messing about with the camera.

'Oi!' demanded Penyghent, stomping in two hours later, 'haven't you lot finished with the camera yet?'

'Er, no,' said Great Nab, covered in gunge and with bracken on his head, 'we're still, like, working on the plot.'

'Give over!' said Penyghent as they started messing about again. 'It's *our* turn now...you're just messing about!'

'Smile!' said Small Nab, pointing the camera at her, 'we're making a documentary called *Bossy Chicks!*'

Penyghent snatched the camera. 'Don't call me 'chick'!' she growled and stalked off.

As soon as the *Yo-o TV* team realised the *Sensible TV* team were being really serious and writing schedules and having actual ideas, they thought they'd better do the same. Then they realised they hadn't a clue how to do all that, and sent Yockenthwaite out to see if he could snoop on what the others were up to.

Soon both Troll teams were being incredibly secretive and holding meetings in strange, hidden places – while at the same time sending out spies. All very silly, because they were spending all their time trying to earwig what the others were planning and not preparing any programmes of their own...

'Did y'hear what they've got on at 8 o'clock, Yockenthwaite?' asked Great Nab.

'Yeah, I think it's a programme called *Don't Say Anything – I Think That Bobble-Hatted Prat Is Listening.*'

'Sounds interesting,' said Askrigg.

'The judging of the TV programmes will take place,' announced King Roger, 'this evening!'

'AAAARGH!!' screamed Askrigg.

'PANIC!' yelled Great Nab.

So everyone shot off and started filming at 90 miles per hour and *just* got all their sample programmes ready by the time King Roger said:

'OK, sit down and be quiet, and let's roll the first film.'

Roger flicked a switch on the projector (which, like the camera, he'd borrowed from his step-dad) and onto the screen (ditto) came the *Sensible Television* logo. This was followed by snippets of a programme called *Newsfile* – '...a formal, yet lively discussion of the day's events...' another one called *Word of the Week* – '...our intelligence test, where panellists have to guess the meaning of difficult words that aren't even in the dictionary...' and ended up with Penyghent doing the weather forecast.

This was *so* gripping that the Nab Twins, Yockenthwaite and Askrigg all fell asleep and had to be woken up with a pointed stick by Roger so they could watch their own film. This opened with a loud raspberry noise, some plinky music and a programme called *Name That Foot* (loads of sirens and major amounts of gunge), which was followed by a soap opera called *The Flying Gunge Doctors* and finished with Great Nab, dressed as a chicken, doing a 20-second weather report.

This was so genuinely appalling that Aysgarth, Penyghent, Kettlewell and Trucklecrag all sat in a horrified silence until the film ended.

'You can't put rubbish like that on every night, King Roger!' exclaimed Penyghent, when she finally found her voice.

'Yes you can!' said Small Nab. 'It's fun – yours is just *boring!*'

'Look,' sighed Roger, 'you've *both* got it wrong. TV should be fun *and* informative, not just all one or the other. Look, you lot at *Serious*

Television go away and make something that's thoughtful and a little more fun...and you lot at *Yo-o Radical Television* go away and make something that's fun and a little more thoughtful.'

Which is what they did. Sort of. As King Roger found when he popped in on *Yo-o Radical Television*'s cave the next day.

'What're you making?' he asked Great Nab.
  'A programme called *Politics Today*,' he replied.
  'Sounds a bit more serious...great, mind if I watch a bit?' said Roger. Askrigg arranged himself at a desk and turned to ask Yockenthwaite a question.
  'So, Yockenthwaite,' he said, 'do you think, in view of the current government position on agricultural subsidies, an entry into Europe would be a good or bad thing?'
  There was a pause, while Yockenthwaite scratched his head like a bloke off the news.
  'A bad thing,' replied Yockenthwaite.
  '*Wrong!*' squealed Askrigg, as lights started to flash, sirens howled...and half a ton of gunge fell on Yockenthwaite's head.
  'Oh-oh...I don't think you've quite understood the concept...' groaned Roger.

He was about to try and explain the concept when Penyghent came rushing in.

'King Roger – you've got to help, it's Dad, he's in trouble!'

It appeared that Aysgarth and the *Sensible Television* programme makers hadn't quite grasped the concept, either. Out on the moor Roger found Aysgarth wearing bunny ears and swinging upside down, like a pendulum, from a large wooden frame.

'He's being a Swinging Weather Rabbit...' explained Penyghent.

'We thought it'd liven things up a bit if, instead of just standing in front of a map, he threw weather symbols at it dressed as a bunny,' added Kettlewell.

The *Radical Television* team stood and watched Aysgarth in what you could only call 'full swing'. They were gobsmacked at the sight.

'Yo-o!' said Yockenthwaite, enthusiastically.

'Radical!' agreed Great Nab, as Roger stopped Aysgarth swinging and got him back on the ground again.

'Are you thinking what I'm thinking?' Small Nab asked his brother, as it occurred to him that there had to be a game in this *somewhere*.

'Swinging Gunge Skittles?' queried Great Nab.

'Exactly!' grinned Small Nab.

And so all the Rottentrolls began playing the *fantastic* new game of Swinging Gunge Skittles, which entailed someone swinging upside-down and throwing gunge-filled balloons at a line of Trolls standing on rocks. It was so fantastic, in fact, that they forgot all about making television programmes, or even watching TV. Which was a good thing, because while they were playing, Commander Harris mended his satellite dish so it stopped picking up TV and went back to being just an ordinary radar receiver again.

Actually, they were so engrossed in their new pastime that none of them bothered going back to the command hut.

Until Commander Harris worked out how to plug in a video game, that is...

PART 3 (The Miners' Strike)

If you want my opinion (and even if you don't), the person who invented teenagers should be taken outside and given a good talking to. I mean, what *can* they have been thinking of? Maybe I'm just getting a bit too old, but I think all teenagers should be put in a zoo until they're not teenagers any more.

The extraordinary thing is that while just about everything in Troller's Ghyll is completely different to the outside world, when it comes to teenagers – by which here I mean the Nab Twins – it's *horribly* similar. All these two ever seem to do is go round saying 'radical' (which means 'great'), shouting *CATTLE G-R-I-D!!* (which is the name of their appalling rock band) and practising silly handshakes. Oh, and complaining bitterly whenever anyone asks them to do *anything*. Like, if Asygarth were to say something such as:

'Can you collect some water?'

Great Nab would say:

'*AH-HHHH!* It's *always* us, innit,' and then hit something.

And Small Nab would say:

'*Every* time, always us...' and hit something else. Now, if it really were true that it was *always* them, you could understand the Twins getting a bit annoyed...but it wasn't true. In fact, if you made a garlic pasty-style pie chart of all the jobs that needed doing in Troller's Ghyll and divided it up according to the amount of jobs done by each Rottentroll, then everyone's bit would be approximately the same size...except for the Nab Twins, whose slice would be so small you'd need a scanning electron microscope to see it. Truth to tell, they only really had one job, which was collecting wood.

Every morning they'd go to the Storiths Wood to collect firewood, a task that only took an hour a day, if that. But they loved it because they spent precisely three minutes collecting wood and the next 57 minutes rehearsing their appalling pop band.

Now you know how people often say that something's so bad it's good? Well, Cattle Grid were a whole other level of 'bad'. In fact the very first time they'd played, Aysgarth had said, very firmly:

'One more note out of that eclectic guitar in *this* valley, and it goes into the skip, along with the drums!'

Which, ordinarily, would've been the end of it for the Nab Twins and their dreams of being the next big thing in the charts. Except they had the only job in the valley which allowed anyone to go out of the valley, up past Commander Harris's small toll booth.

'Morning lads,' he'd say to the Twins every morning, as they passed by dragging a large bag containing their instruments. 'What's in the bag today, then? Grass cuttings, same as usual?'

'Yeah, boss,' Great Nab would snigger, 'grass cuttings.'

'S'right, man,' Small Nab would cackle, 'it's compost!'

'Nothing gets past me, you know!' said Commander Harris every morning, letting the Twins out of the valley.

As soon as they were in the woods the Twins would go completely berserk and rush round picking up anything remotely woody for a couple of minutes before setting up their instruments – Great Nab's drumkit and Small Nab's guitar.

The only songs they knew were the ones they'd heard on King Roger's collection of hiss-filled tapes, played through his rather ancient and not very good personal stereo, and there was only one word to describe their versions of them. Terrible. The two of them would start by shouting:

'ONE! TWO! A-ONE-TWO-THREE-*FOUR!*'

...just like the groups on the tapes. But, unlike the groups, they'd then immediately stop and Small Nab would try and work out where his fingers should go on the guitar, while his brother would have to find the drum sticks he'd thrown over his shoulders. This ritual was usually followed by some loud squabbling over whether the words were right, a bit of to-ing and fro-ing about what order the chords should go in (Small Nab had learnt three, so there was actually something to argue about) and finally ended with a bit of a dust-up. So, you see, everything was just fine and dandy. The Rottentrolls got their firewood, the Nab Twins got to fool around *and* look like they were pulling their weight, and the valley was a wonderful place...until King Roger Becket decided to improve it. You'd think he'd have learnt...

'I've noticed that your fires keep going out,' he said, putting a small fan heater on the table in the Great Cave, 'so I got you one of these – it'll save you from having to collect all that fire-wood every day!'

The Nab Twins were less than delighted, in fact they were horrified. So horrified that they completely lost the power of speech for a moment or two, which was nice.

'That's lovely, King Roger,' smiled Penyghent, 'but the only thing is...it's electric.'

'Yeah!' said Great Nab, recovering quickly as he spotted a way out of his and Small Nab's predicament. 'Yeah, right man – we've got nowhere to plug it in!'

'Shame,' grinned Small Nab, picking the heater up and throwing it over his shoulder.

'Oi – hold on!' said Roger. 'There are other ways of getting electricity than just out of plug sockets you know!'

Roger got up. Everyone followed him out of the cave.

'Are there, King Roger?' asked Penyghent.

'Are there what?'

'Other ways of getting electricity?' said Penyghent.

'Well there must be, mustn't there,' said Roger, 'otherwise how does Commander Harris get all his satellite equipment to work?'

'He gets it in a bag?' offered Great Nab.

'Yeah, like from Electricityland, innit,' added Small Nab.

'Right...from the electricity mines,' Great Nab said, warming to his subject, 'which have all run out...apparently. Which is why firewood is such a *great* idea!'

'Yeah, cos, you know *firewood*, like *grows*, man,' said Small Nab. 'It's organic.'

'What *is* the matter with you two?' said Roger, stopping outside the Commander's hut.

'Er...nuffink,' said the Twins, both looking embarrassed.

'Commander Harris!' waved Roger. 'Listen, I'm teaching this lot about electricity. The Nab Twins think you get yours in a bag from a mine!'

'Mines? I should cocoa NOT!' snorted the Commander. 'Y'don't get electricity from a mine, lads...you must be thinking of zirconium, greyish-white metallic element, atomic number – 40, atomic weight – 91.2, melting point – 1,852 degrees Centigrade!'

'Don't think so,' said Great Nab.

'Y'can't think of things y've never heard of!' said Small Nab.

'I can. I do it all the time,' Yockenthwaite put his hand up. 'Problem is, I can never tell any-one about it afterwards.'

There was a slight pause while everyone thought about this...and then realised it wasn't worth thinking about.

'Shut it, Yockenthwaite!' said Roger, then turned to the Commander. 'So how do you get electricity?'

'Tractor batteries, me laddo.'

'There y'go – batteries!' said Roger. 'That's one way of getting electricity without a plug – a battery is like a little store room of power.'

'And don't go thinking you can make off with any of mine, Your Majesty,' said the Commander. 'If it's electricity you want, why don't you try a dynamo?'

'Brilliant – a *dynamo!* That's *another* way to make electricity...come on lads,' said Roger, turning to leave the hut. 'By the way, Commander, what's 'Jimjam YaHO'?'

'Delayed action Jimjam YaHa,' he replied, casually waving a front leg. 'It takes about sixty seconds to reach its target.'

'That's it then,' sighed Great Nab, once they were all outside the hut. 'What a shame, we're stuck with boring old wood fires...'

'Back to collecting stuff from Storiths Wood...again,' said Small Nab. 'Shame no one's got a dynamo, really...'

'I have!' said Roger brightly.

'WHAT!' howled the Nab Twins.

'The headlamp on my bike works off a dynamo!'

You could've knocked the Nab Twins over with a feather, and everything went quiet. Except for the sheep standing next to them, which suddenly went BAAAAaaaaa! and soared up in the air, being as it was the target for Commander Harris's Jimjam YaHO.

'OK, here we go!' said Roger, sitting astride his Road Wizard bike, with Slipstream AirMaster sports wheels and a saddle that looked like a liquorice ice lolly. This was set up so its wheels were off the ground and he could peddle like a madman. A couple of twisted wires went from the little dynamo thingy on the back wheel, across the cave floor to the fan heater.

'Y'see, it works like this,' Roger explained as his legs pumped up and down so fast you could hardly see them. 'The wheels go round, which turns the dynamo, which sends electricity down the wires, and – *BINGO!*'

Suddenly, and as if by magic – by which I mean *real* magic, the stuff that actually works, not the sort that Trucklecrag does, which doesn't... work, that is – the fan heater started blasting out hot air like nobody's business.

Everyone was phenomenally impressed. Well, almost everyone. Not long after the heater began working a loud chanting noise could be heard coming from outside the cave.

'What's going on?' asked Roger, coming out of the Great Cave to find the Nab Twins standing by a glowing brazier, Small Nab holding a large placard reading: SUPPORT THE TGWU! and Great Nab a banner saying much the same.

'T-G-W-U! ASK YOURSELF WHICH SIDE ARE YOU!' yelled the Twins.

'Hold on, what's the TGWU?' said Roger, looking puzzled.

'It stands for the Troller's Ghyll Woodcutters Union,' said Great Nab.

'What's a union?' enquired Askrigg.

'I know,' said Yockenthwaite, 'it's a...'

'NO IT'S NOT!' interrupted everyone else.

'Fair enough,' said Yockenthwaite.

'A union,' Great Nab said the word so it sounded like 'you-knee-on'. 'It's what you call it when a load of people, who all do the same kind of job, sort of decide they're going to join together in a big gang, like.'

'Gang?' sniffed Penyghent. 'Gangs are what people like Yockenthwaite have!'

'Yo-o!' grinned Yockenthwaite.

'Grown-up people, who have jobs, don't belong to gangs.'

'They do have 'em,' protested Small Nab.

'It's like school...in the playground,' agreed Great Nab, 'if you're not very big and someone pushes you around, then you can't do much.'

'BUT!' said Small Nab, grabbing his brother and pulling him close, 'if all the Not Very Big People join together, they look more, like, *awesome*...and other people think twice about doin' things that'll make 'em miserable.'

'So what's making you two so miserable?' asked Penyghent.

'The *evil*...' hissed Small Nab

'The *what?*'

'The evil of *electricity!*' Small Nab hissed louder.

'We don't need it, man,' nodded Great Nab. 'Y'can *see* fire! Y'can *smell* it!'

'And y'can get the smoke in your eyes and they go out all the time!' said Aysgrath.

'But we *know* wood, man,' said Great Nab, persuasively.

'Yeah,' agreed Small Nab, 'and, like, no one knows the side-effects of that fan heater thingy, do they? Exactly what will it do to future Rottentroll generations?'

'Side-effects?' snorted Roger. 'There aren't any 'side-effects' from a fan heater – it's *completely* safe!'

'Well you would say that, wouldn't you,' said great Nab. 'It's *your* fan heater, innit.'

'Let's face it,' beamed Penyghent, 'the fan heater is cleaner, quieter...and it also blow-dries your hair!'

'Check out me kinky afro!' chortled Sigsworthy Crags, who was waving a fishing umbrella around for no apparent reason at all. But then, that was Sigsworthy Crags for you – mad as a hatter and now sporting a hair style that looked like he'd just stuck his fingers in a wall socket.

'Hands up who wants to keep the fan heater!' shouted Penyghent.

A forest – or possibly a small copse – of hands shot up.

'And hands up who wants to stick with the old-fashioned wood fires!'

Four hands shot up...all belonging to the Nab Twins.

'Sorry, lads,' Penyghent smiled sweetly, 'it's just...well, it's just progress!'

Except the Nab Twins weren't going to have 'progress'. Oh no. They couldn't *stop* people from using the new fan heater, but they *could* hang around the cave entrance all day trying to make them feel horribly guilty about what they were doing. All their shouting and banner waving and placard thrusting and name calling, however, just made everyone get extremely fed up.

Inside the cave Roger had organised everyone into a bike-peddling rota so there would be constant power for the fan heater.

'Hurts your legs after a bit, this,' said Kettlewell, '*and* your arms!'

'Two more minutes, and then it's Askrigg's turn,' said Roger, trying to ignore the shouts of '*SUPPORT THE TGWU!*' and '*WOOD IS GOOD – ELECTRICITY IS*...er, what rhymes with electricity?' from outside the cave.

'It's *great*, this fan heater, King Roger,' said Penyghent.

'Certainly is,' agreed Aysgarth. 'The only thing spoiling it is the racket from those two *berks* outside.'

Now Roger knew that he could easily have waited until the Nab Twins eventually got bored and went off to do something else, as is the way with teenagers, but a little voice in his head told him that wasn't what good Kings did. Kings went out and spoke to their subjects and explained things to them.

'Now look here, lads, electricity's a good thing, y'know.'

'No it's not, man, it's *evil*,' said Great Nab, waving his placard. 'It's evil, dangerous and *rotten!*'

'Right!' nodded Small Nab. 'Nothing good's *ever* come out of electricity!'

'Really? How about rock music?' said Roger.

'Eh?' said the Nab Twins.

'All those tapes I lend you...how d'you think the bands make their instruments work?' asked Roger.

'That's...*electricity?*' said Great Nab.

'Absolutely...electric guitars, electric synthesisers – even electric *drums* sometimes,' said Roger. 'And you like all that stuff, don't you?'

This astounding information stopped the Nab

Twins dead in their tracks. You could almost hear the cogs in their brains working overtime to make sense of what they'd just been told. And then Small Nab sighed a huge sigh and threw his banner into the tin brazier...

'Yeah, well that's it, innit? We only agreed to go wood collecting so's we could get away from the wrinklies and practise *our* rock band,' he admitted.

'*You've* got a rock band?' said Roger.

'Yeah, man,' said Great Nab, ''s called Cattle Grid, innit.'

At which point the Nab Twins started playing imaginary guitars and making loads of squealing feedback noises. King Roger suddenly realised that the Nab twins weren't protesting about wood being better than electricity. They were *actually* protesting about being forced to stop doing something they liked.

So, as a good King, Roger had a long think about progress and change and all that stuff, and wondered if there wasn't a way in which he could keep everyone in Troller's Ghyll happy. It took a bit of time because, although he was a good King, he wasn't a phenomenally bright one, but eventually – after tripping over the old fishing umbrella Sigsworthy Crags had left lying around – Roger came up with an idea...

'Rottentrolls and trollslips,' Roger announced, 'I hereby declare the very first Rottentroll wind-farm – *OPEN!*'

The fishing umbrella had been turned into a tatty but very efficient windmill. It stood in the tin brazier the Nab Twins had used when they'd been on strike and wires ran from it into the Great Cave.

'Here we see the wind *turning* the blades,' said Roger, 'which in turn rotates the dynamo in the barrel, which makes the electricity which powers the fan heater – and no more aching legs from pedalling!'

Huge cheers all round, and much throwing of hats into the air...

'The only other thing is,' Roger put his hand up, 'it's going to need oiling every day to keep it running smoothly...and so I appoint, as Official Windfarm Maintenance Engineers – the Nab Twins!'

And so it was that the Rottentrolls got to keep their beloved fan heater, Sigsworthy Crags got to keep his kinky afro hairdo, and, for an hour a day, a distant part of Troller's Ghyll was alive once again with the sound of music. Or, more precisely, with the sound of Cattle Grid, which isn't the same thing at all.

Chapter 4 (The Gambling Crisis)

It was Monday. And what always happens on a Monday? In case you haven't been paying attention it's when King Roger has his lesson in the ancient marital...sorry spellchecker malfunction...martial art of Jimjam YaHa from Commander Harris. Standing on one of Troller's Ghyll's weirdly-shaped rocks, watched by Yockenthwaite, he was practising hard.

'Jimjam YaHa*!!*' he yelled.

'Not bad,' said the Commander. 'Not bad at all.'

'Did I knock that bloke off his picnic?'

'Not actually *off*,' said the Commander, while peering through his binoculars. 'Tragically, you didn't raise your arm high enough, so all you've done is slightly dislodge the corned beef filling in one of his baps.'

'I am *never* going to get this right!' scowled Roger, angrily scooping up his jacket.

'*Courage, mon brave* – better luck next time.'

'King Roger,' said Yockenthwaite, picking something off the ground, 'what's this? It fell out of your pocket.'

'Oh! Er...' said Roger, snatching the pieces of paper back, '...nothing.'

'A-*ha!*' smirked Yockenthwaite. 'That's not allowed, is it?'

'How'd *you* know?'

'I don't,' said Yockenthwaite, 'I just guessed, 'cos you went all shouty.'

'Don't tell anyone.'

'What are they, King Roger?'

'Tickets for next Saturday's National Lottery,' whispered Roger. 'I bought 'em off me bad Uncle Colin with me birthday money.'

'Why shouldn't you have them, King Roger?' asked Yockenthwaite.

'Can't you guess?' frowned Roger, stuffing the tickets back in his pocket. 'Because – surprise, surprise – *adults* say we shouldn't...and d'you know why that is?'

'No,' shrugged Yockenthwaite, 'I don't know anything.'

'Because they don't want children winning. They want to keep all the money for themselves by not letting children win, *that's* why!'

'Is that true?'

'Well I think it is,' said Roger, 'that's why they always say children can't go gambling.'

'What's gambling?' asked Yockenthwaite, innocently...

As you lot should know by now, the answer to that question wasn't going to be as simple as Roger might've liked. To demonstrate what gambling was, he got busy and made a roulette wheel out of an old dustbin lid – the inside of which he'd painted half red and half black – and a ping pong ball, which he then set up in the Great Cave.

'Right,' he said, spinning the lid, 'now I throw in the ping pong ball, wait until the lid stops turning, and see which half it lands in.'

'Roger, King Roger,' said Commander Harris, nodding as he watched the ball land in the red half as the lid stopped spinning.

'Why?' asked Yockenthwaite.

'Well...if – before I spun it – I'd said the ball was going to land in the red half, I'd've won some money,' explained Roger. 'And if I'd said it was going to land in the black, I'd've lost some.'

'Really?' beamed Yockenthwaite.

'That's basically what gambling is...trying to win money by guessing what will happen in the future,' said Roger. 'And if my numbers are the ones chosen in next Saturday's National Lottery, I'll have enough money to buy a big car and go round the world – so *THRRRRRP!!* to the grown ups!'

And with that King Roger went home. And Yockenthwaite went home. And the Commander went...rather strange. He stayed in the Great Cave, spinning the dustbin lid and throwing the ping pong ball in for quite a while.

'RED...RED...*RED!!*' he yelled at the spinning lid. 'Come on Betsy, for your daddy-o – do it for your old – *YES, YES YES!!*'

In fact, the Commander didn't go home for absolutely *ages*.

'BLACK, BLACK, *BLACK!!* Come on old girl...land in the bla – AARGH!! No-no *NO!*'

As the night wore on the Commander started eating grass (always a bad sign) and drinking far too much water (a sign he was on a losing streak of major proportions).

'C'mon, *c'mon!!* Let's make it the best of six thousand, eh? Best of six thousand...I'm going for the red, big bright lucky red...Do it for daddy-o, just *one* red...just – *AARGH!!*'

I suppose it mightn't be a bad idea if I explained something here. You see, while Commander Harris was in the Far East as the mascot of the King's Fusiliers, there was, how shall I put it, an incident.

The Commander had been taken prisoner by some desperately inscrutable enemy sheep on the Kwong-Hak River in the Northern Province. They kept him in a bamboo hut for ages and made him play a terrible game called Welsh Roulette. Now you may never have heard of it, but it's a psychological nightmare. Someone secretly shakes up a can of fizzy-pop, puts three identical cans in front of the victim and – under threat of a good slapping – makes them choose one and then open it under their nose.

These dastardly enemy sheep made the Commander play the game again and again and again, and by the time he escaped – on a raft of empty fizzy-pop tins, as it happens – he was completely addicted to its terrible thrills. He'd managed to keep his ghastly need for gambling excitement under control for 40 years...until, that is, King Roger had mentioned the National Lottery and made the dustbin lid roulette wheel.

From that moment the Commander was a different man. He took over an empty cave in the valley, stuck a big neon sign outside saying 'Lucky Dip Casino' and stood outside wearing a dinner jacket, smoking a cigar and hustling for business...

'Lucky, lucky, *LUCKEEE!!*' he shouted.

'What's a casino?' asked Yockenthwaite.

'A casino?' grinned the Commander. 'Why it's a house of fun, lad...a place of entertainment – why not step right in and find out for yourself?'

'OK!' said Yockenthwaite.

'What's it to be, laydeez and gennulmen?' said the Commander, puffing a huge smoke ring. 'Blackjack? Pontoon? Bagatelle?'

'I don't understand what any of those words mean,' said Aysgarth.

'No matter, sir,' said the Commander, spinning the dustbin lid. 'Why not try your hand at roulette? Put your money down, sir, and watch the ball. Round and round she goes, where she stops no one knows...'

'No! Look, Commander, I'm *completely* opposed to all this,' frowned Aysgarth. 'Socially, morally, ethically...'

'Number 12!' said the Commander.

'Twelve? That's *my* number!' screamed Aysgarth. 'HA-*HA!* Eat my dirt you losers – and I'll have 20 quid on red 42!'

And so it was that the Rottentrolls became hooked on gambling. They all went betting mad – rolling dice till the cows came home...playing roulette till the cows went back again – they all spent *all* their time and *all* their money down at Commander Harris's Lucky Dip Casino and everyone very quickly picked up how to gamble. Well, *almost* everyone...

'Here's your cards,' said the Commander, expertly dealing out five cards.

'Oh *no!*' yelled Great Nab when he saw his.

'I'll buy one,' said Aysgarth.

'Bust,' moaned Great Nab.

'19!' grinned Aysgarth, putting his cards down.

'20!' said Askrigg, spreading his cards on the table.

'Mr Bun the Baker!' said Yockenthwaite.

'What?' frowned the Commander.

'I've brought my own cards,' said Yockenthwaite, 'those are a bit boring...'

'Ooooh!' said Yockenthwaite, as he got up and dusted himself down. He decided, there and then, he wouldn't go back into the casino out of which he'd just been thrown, unceremoniously. He'd start his *own* casino. Which was when King Roger came back into the valley to check up on his subjects and found himself staring at something called the 'You'll Definitely Win In Here Casino'. Otherwise known as Yockenthwaite's cave...

'Hello,' said Roger, 'anybody there?'

'Aha! A customer!' replied Yockenthwaite, poking his head round the cave entrance. 'Roll up, roll up! Lucky, lucky, luckee! Place your bets for Slug Roulette!'

'What's Slug Roulette?' asked Roger, following Yockenthwaite into his cave.

'Stationary, stationary, stationary she sits,' intoned Yockenthwaite, pointing at a sluggy-type thing in the middle of a circle of card he'd divided up into six fairly equal coloured slices. 'Which way she'll move nobody can predict!'

'Yockenthwaite, that's an old jelly baby!'

'Is it?' said Yockenthwaite. 'Oh *pig!* I've been watching that for three days!'

'What on earth is this 'casino' thing, Yockenthwaite?' asked Roger.

'Well I got kicked out of the other one, so I had to make me own,' explained Yockenthwaite.

'What *other* one?'

At which point King Roger ran out of Yockenthwaite's cave, round the corner and into the Lucky Dip Casino.

'What's going on here?' demanded Roger, bursting into the gaudily decorated cave.

'Shhhh!' said the assembled crowd of Rottentrolls as Commander Harris let the ball go, watched it bounce round the dustbin lid and land.

'It's 28 black!' he cried.

'Rats!' went everyone, except Little Strid, who'd won.

'Why's the floor all covered in thousands of crisp packets!' asked Roger.

'That was my dinner, man,' said Small Nab.

'And breakfast,' added Great Nab.

'Lunch, tea, in-between-meal snacks...' said Aysgarth, not taking his eyes off the roulette wheel for a moment.

'No one's been home since this place opened,' muttered Penyghent. 'Roll 'em, Commander – I'll bet my entire tool kit on 24 red!'

'Right!' shouted Roger, snatching the ping pong ball away. 'This place is closed down – and I hereby declare that casinos aren't allowed anywhere in Troller's Ghyll!'

Tragically, just like Commander Harris, all the Rottentrolls had become completely addicted to the excitement of gambling...and, if you don't already know, the thing that happens the moment you make something illegal is that it goes underground.

Which meant that when Roger went looking for someone to play football with, he couldn't find a single person. But in the distance he could hear music playing...

'Right. That's *definitely* it!' shouted Roger, as he burst into a secret hidey-hole in the bracken, grabbing the little snail racetrack the Rottentrolls were using to bet on. 'My valley should be a place of peace and happiness – you lot've made it a den of gambling!'

'Don't get holier-than-thou, matey boy,' sniffed Commander Harris. 'What's *that* in your pocket?'

'D'you mean me lottery ticket?'

'Exactly!' said Aysgarth. 'Kings have to set an example, King Roger. Either it's OK to gamble, or it isn't. So what's it to be – right or wrong?'

'Twenty quid says it's wrong!' said the Commander.

'You're on!' replied Aysgarth, and they both slapped money down on a rock.

'STOP IT!' shouted Roger, who then stopped himself. This was a *very* tricky question and he had to think very hard to try and work out the right answer. 'OK, OK, ' he said finally, 'you can't say it's *completely* wrong to gamble, because lots of people enjoy it...but what is wrong is getting hooked on doing it too much, because that stops you having a normal life. Like it has with you lot.'

'Yeah, great,' said Penyghent. 'But how d'you make sure you do it just enough to not get hooked?'

'I – I don't know, Penyghent,' Roger sat down on a rock. 'To be honest, I don't think anyone knows...perhaps it's just when you get older you get more grown up about it,' Roger looked at his lottery ticket. 'Maybe...'

And so it was that on Sunday, after the National Lottery draw, Roger came into the valley...

'Yo-o, King Roger!' said Yockenthwaite when he saw him. 'How did it go? Are you going to be able to buy that big car and travel round the world?'

'Yup.'

'What – you won the lottery?'

'No,' said Roger. 'I sold the tickets back to me bad uncle Colin, went down the Oxfam shop and bought a guitar...I'm gonna join a band, become a rock'n'roll star and make shedloads of money!'

'He-hey!!' yelled the Nab Twins. '*CATTLE GRI-I-I-I-I-I-D!*'

And so it was that King Roger joined the Nab Twins, appalling rock band, played all the wrong chords and got mixed up in all their fights about who was worst.

And so it also was that Commander Harris turned his roulette wheel into another satellite dish and the valley went back to being its normal, quiet and peaceful place...although I bet it doesn't stay that way for long.

In fact I'll bet you 50p...

PART 5 (The Art Gallery)

The trouble started, as it always seems to do in Troller's Ghyll, with a chance remark by Roger. This time he just happened to mention that he probably wouldn't be coming to the valley the next day because he was going on a school trip to an art gallery.

'A what-whatery?' asked Yockenthwaite, who knew less than nothing about almost everything – except, just possibly, playing Rat-Up-A-Drainpipe.

'An *art* gallery,' repeated Roger. 'You know... it's a big hall where they hang paintings so that everyone can walk round and look at them.'

'*Do* they now?' said Aysgarth, rattling his pipe on his teeth. 'Do they really? Hmmmm...'

Now, y'see Aysgarth had a little secret. He'd always fancied himself as a bit of an artist, and

from time to time he would paint pictures of the valley and the sheep and the mad rocks. At night he dreamed of being told how good they were by serious-looking people on television... people who talked like they had a mouth full of hot peanuts and said things like 'It has an essential tree-ish-ness that just says unmistakably "I am a tree – there is absolutely no way I could be a bridge or a cat"', while everyone nodded as if they knew what they were on about.

So it wasn't surprising that, after hearing what King Roger was up to, Aysgarth decided the Rottentrolls should build...

'An *art* gallery?' said Kettlewell.

'That's right,' said Aysgarth. 'We'll knock through an extension to the Great Cave and turn it into the first ever Rottentroll Art Gallery!'

'But we haven't got any paintings, Dad!' said Penyghent.

'We will soon,' grinned Aysgarth. 'Everyone's going to paint one! Chop, chop – off y'go! By tomorrow night I want a painting from every *single* Rottentroll!'

Everyone looked at each other, and then rushed off in all directions to grab paints, brushes and paper. And then there was a pause in the hectic activity as everyone stopped and had a little think about what it was they were going to paint...always a good idea when it comes to doing pictures.

In the end Penyghent painted some flowers, which wasn't a bad effort at all; Kettlewell did a picture of a garlic pasty, decided she didn't like it, decked it and painted another one. And the Nab Twins came up with the whizzy notion to paint each other, by which I mean they slapped blue paint on each other's faces, and then they did an appalling version of their appalling band's logo.

On and on it went. Trucklecrag did someone doing magic, Askrigg produced a picture of an American football (*just* the ball...) and Little Strid painted a house. Blacksyke, naturally, went off in a huff to read back issues of her favourite celebrity magazine – *Bog Off*.

And then there was Yockenthwaite. Now there was a problem with Yockenthwaite doing pictures, mainly stemming from the fact that he was by far the stupidest of the Rottentrolls. He'd seen Aysgarth painting, seen him with his arm outstretched and his thumb stuck up, which normally, as *anyone* would know, meant he was measuring things in real life against his thumb so he'd get them the right size in the

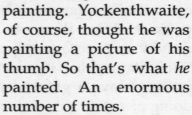

painting. Yockenthwaite, of course, thought he was painting a picture of his thumb. So that's what *he* painted. An enormous number of times.

'This is going to be the thumb to end all thumbs,' he muttered to himself as he admired his umpteenth version. 'This is going to be the best thumb in the whole world...It's going to be the *Mona Thumba*.'

Yockenthwaite mixed and mixed and mixed his paints on his square palette until he'd got the colour just right...but by then, tragically, he'd completely run out of paint. And, even more tragically, he'd also run out of time.

'Time's up!' shouted Aysgarth.

'What?' squeaked Yockenthwaite. 'No, just a minute...hold on...y'can't...'

'All paintings into the Great Cave, Rottentrolls and trollslips!' shouted Aysgarth.

'No...*please!*' pleaded Yockenthwaite, 'I haven't...'

But it was too late. Everyone, including King Roger went into the Great Cave, where there was a brand new hole in one of the walls.

'The art gallery's going to be in there, is it?' asked Roger, poking his head through the hole.

'That's right,' nodded Aysgarth proudly. 'And here are all the paintings to go in it!'

'Oh wow!' gasped Roger, staring at the row of pictures lined up against the wall, ready for hanging. 'Who did *that* one?'

'Thank you. Very kind, King Roger,' smiled Aysgarth. 'That was me, yes...I worked quite hard on getting the stippled feel on them rocks on the left...'

'No, I'm sorry, Aysgarth,' said Roger, 'I meant *that* one behind you. With all the squiggles on it.'

'I'm sorry...I'm a berk, I know I'm a berk,' moaned Yockenthwaite, hiding behind his mixing palette. 'It's not my fault, I didn't ask to be a berk...please don't hit me with wet bracken!'

'This was you?' asked Roger, amazed.

'I ran out of paint, y'see...and time...' explained Yockenthwaite, 'and everything, I ran out of everything...'

'I *love* it!' said Roger.

'What?' frowned Yockenthwaite. Hardly daring to believe his ears he looked round at the front of his mixing palette.

'It's bright and exciting,' enthused Roger, 'and, oh, I don't know, like fireworks!'

'Fireworks?' mumbled Yockenthwaite, the rusty cogs in his brain creaking into action. 'That's what it is...oh yes...in fact that's the title – *Fireworks*, by Yockenthwaite!'

'Well I think it should have pride of place in the new art gallery!' said Roger.

Now, being the oldest and most important Rottentroll, you'd sort of expect Aysgarth to say something like 'Well done, Yockenthwaite! Isn't it *great* King Roger likes your painting best?' But just because you're old, it doesn't stop you from sometimes acting like a baby, so what he *actually* said, after King Roger had left, was: '*WA-AAAAAH!!* Mine's the best! It's miles better than your rubbishy fireworks rubbish! At least *mine* looks like what it's supposed to be...trees and sky and rocks...yours is just a load of *blobs*...'

'King Roger likes it,' smiled Yockenthwaite.

'ONLY BECAUSE HE'S BEING *NICE!*' yelled Aysgarth. 'ONLY COS HE KNOWS YOU CAN'T *PAINT!* ONLY COS HE'S TAKING *PITY* ON YOU COS YOU CAN'T PAINT SOMETHING THAT *LOOKS* LIKE ANY-THING!'

Well, what can I say? After an outburst like that even Picasso would've had second thoughts about his choice of career, so you can imagine what it did to someone as dim as Yockenthwaite, who couldn't even *spell* career.

He was so sad...sadder than a Christmas cracker without any bang...sadder than a clown who gets lost in the rain going to a children's party, loses all his balloons and then gets shout-ed at by his Mum when he gets home. Which, you have to admit, is about as sad as it gets.

'It *is* rubbish,' wailed Yockenthwaite, mooching round the Great Cave on his own. 'Aysgarth's right...he must be, he's the oldest Rottentroll. I must be a berk – a rubbish-painting-painter of a *BERK!*'

Yockenthwaite picked his painting up and threw it over his shoulder. Where it sailed through the air, bounced off a wall and disappeared through the hole into the new gallery extension.

'Oh 'eck...' said Yockenthwaite when he realised what had happened.

Grabbing a torch, Yockenthwaite climbed through the hole to get his rubbish-painting back...and stepped straight onto it. But as he bent down to pick it up he saw something on the wall. It was a painting of a bull. Swinging the torch around he saw another bull. And then another bull...in fact a whole stampede of bulls all being chased by men with spears. The painting was *massive*, covering the whole wall of the new extension.

'Ha-*hay!*' said Yockenthwaite. 'Yo-o!'

Which basically meant that he'd had an idea.

Which was good, except that with Yockenthwaite an idea is like a dustbin lorry with no brakes going down a very steep slope. It moves very fast, you can't stop it and you just *know* it's going to end up a load of rubbish.

'Now *this* painting definitely looks like something,' muttered Yockenthwaite, working his idea out. 'So why don't I just sign it and pretend I did it?'

So that's what he did. But he couldn't leave well enough alone...

'Only there's just *one* thing wrong with it,' he said, looking at the painting that wasn't his. 'It needs a bit of cheering up. I'll just get me paints...'

The next day, when Roger came into the valley, he found a large banner, reading 'ROTTEN-TROLL ART GALLERY' hanging over the entrance to the Great Cave.

'Are we ready then, Aysgarth?' he said.

'All present and correct for installing the pictures in the new art gallery, King Roger,' beamed Aysgarth as he ushered Roger into the Great Cave extension. 'Now I think if we're...ha-ha-ha...*seriously* presuming that my picture is best it should go at the far end...*WHAT!!?'*

'What's this?' whispered Roger, eyes out on stalks as he saw the pictures covering the walls.

'Yo-o! It's me painting!' said Yockenthwaite. 'It's called *Cowboys and Indians* by Yockenthwaite. These are the cowboys with the guns going *acka-acka-acka* and they've been ambushed by the Indians with the woo-ooo headdresses and *that* one's got a lawnmower cos I tried to draw a spear but it didn't work out so I had to change it...and they're saying "No, no, cowboys – you not steal our heap lovely buffalo, we come and *pee-yow!* with our arrows..."'

'Yockenthwaite...' said Roger.

'Pee-yowww! Acka-acka-acka! "No, no, you not having our buffalo, pardners, they're happy with us!"...see, I made the buffalo look happy...and then the brush slipped...'

'Yockenthwaite...' Roger said again.

'And then it went all red, so I made it into a jumper. And then I had to make *all* the buffalo have jumpers...'

'YOCKENTHWAITE!'

'Yes...?' said Yockenthwaite.

'This painting was on the wall already, wasn't it?'

'NO! No-no-no-no!' protested Yockenthwaite. 'No-no-no-no...Yes!'

'Oh *no-o-o-o!!'* moaned Roger.

'What's the matter, King Roger?' asked Penyghent.

'I've seen some things like these in the gallery,' explained Roger, pointing at the wall. 'They're prehistoric paintings!'

'What's 'prehistoric', man?' asked Great Nab.

'Old,' said Roger. 'Very old.'

'Older that Phil Collins?' enquired Small Nab.

'*Thousands* of years old,' sighed Roger.

'Wow-w-w!' said Great Nab, impressed. 'Phil Collins's *dad!*'

'Cavemen painted these pictures!' shouted Roger. 'They painted all the stuff they did in the day on their cave walls!'

'And that's what these are?' asked Penyghent, looking at a 'caveman', which was now an 'Indian' with a lawnmower.

'Yes – and they're very, *very* rare!' said Roger. 'This is a painting of cavemen hunting buffalo, and Yockenthwaite's turned them into cowboys and Indians and put *jumpers* on all the buffalo!'

'IT'S NOT FAIR!' wailed Yockenthwaite all of a sudden.

Everyone went quiet.

'I only wanted to make a painting that *looked* like something, because Aysgarth said "only a painting that looks like what it's meant to be is a proper painting".'

'Aysgarth?' said Roger, turning ominously.

'I, er...er...' stuttered Aysgarth. 'Well, it was *rubbish*, his painting, King Roger.'

'It wasn't rubbish, it was modern art,' said Roger. 'I saw loads of paintings at the gallery exactly like that!'

'Well then modern art is rubbish!' snorted Aysgarth. 'Yockenthwaite's painting didn't look a bit like fireworks!'

'But it made me *think* of fireworks, Aysgarth!' said Roger. 'And that's all that matters. And now, because you don't like modern art, he's destroyed some very *old* art.'

'What d'you think we should do, King Roger?' asked Penyghent.

And so it was that King Roger decided that he should very *carefully* wipe all the googly eyes and jumpers and lawnmowers off the cave paintings, seal up the Rottentroll Art Gallery extension to keep it safe and have an outdoor gallery instead. In which the pride of place would go to *Fireworks*, by Yockenthwaite.

And while Aysgarth never actually learnt to *like* Yockenthwaite's painting, at least he sort of began to understand that there wasn't a 'right' or a 'wrong' way to paint a picture.

'So, King Roger...' said Yockenthwaite, as they

walked down the valley, 'does that mean anything that makes you think of something is 'art'?'

'S'pose so.'

'Which means *anything* could be art, then,' said Yockenthwaite, 'like trees, because they make me think of waves sometimes?'

'Well, not trees, because no one actually *made* trees...except God, possibly,' said Roger, picking at the bracken. 'Y've got to have *made* something for it to be art.'

'Like what I've just trod in?' asked Yockenthwaite. 'Cos someone 'made' those, didn't they?'

'Yockenthwaite...'

'And they make me think of...'

'*Yockenthwaite!*'

'...chocolate raisins...'

'Yockenthwaite, shall we stop talking about art?' said Roger. 'We've had enough for today. Let's talk about something less complicated.'

'OK,' said Yockenthwaite as they walked round the Rumble Rock and down towards the dying sun. 'Who's 'God'?'

PART 6 (The Football Sponsorship Scandal)

Of all the Rottentrolls there was only one who could be called remotely sensible: Penyghent. In fact, if you did a computer diagram of Penyghent's brain and told the computer to shade in the 'sensible' bits it'd look...well, it'd look like this:

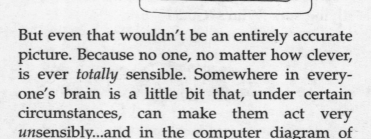

But even that wouldn't be an entirely accurate picture. Because no one, no matter how clever, is ever *totally* sensible. Somewhere in everyone's brain is a little bit that, under certain circumstances, can make them act very *un*sensibly...and in the computer diagram of

Penyghent's brain it would be a tiny wee red dot – just about as big as:

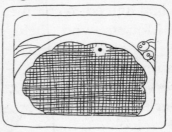

But there, all the same.

The circumstances that made Penyghent act as daft as Yockenthwaite occurred when King Roger turned up in the valley one day with a football...

'I know what that is! I know that!' said Yockenthwaite, pointing at it. 'It's a...it's a...what's that then?'

'No one seen one of these before?' asked Roger.

'I know, I know!' said Yockenthwaite, jumping up and down. 'It's a globe of a planet where all the countries are the same shape!'

'It's a football,' sighed Roger.

'I knew that.'

'And we're going to play five-a-side!'

Teams were drawn up, kit doled out, laces tied, undone, retied again (especially Yockenthwaite's). And then everyone went off to the flattest piece of ground in the valley to play the match – including Commander Harris, who had agreed to commentate in the style of John Motson, who he'd seen on television once.

'It's a fine afternoon here at the Valley Ground in Troller's Ghyll...let's have a look at the line ups...

'Playing left to right – Aysgarth, Kettlewell, Trucklecrag, Penyghent and King Roger...I'm expecting them to play in Christmas tree formation, allowing King Roger space to move, and probably with Penyghent in goal, what with her being a girlie.

'And playing right to left we've got – Sigsworthy Crags, the Nab Twins (G Nab and S Nab), Yockenthwaite and Askrigg...and the chances are they'll be playing Christmas pudding formation...i.e. following the ball round the field in a dense clump.

'Great atmosphere here, even Blacksyke's turned out with some refreshments, and the official attendance figure is...Little Strid. So that's...one.'

And so it was that the whistle blew and the first ever five-a-side Rottentroll football match kicked off...

'They're away!' Commander Harris yelled into his microphone. 'King Roger finds Trucklecrag wide on the right, running into space – that's a good run from King Roger...oh, sloppy ball, sloppy, *sloppy* return from Trucklecrag, easily headed down by G Nab...who plays it square to S Nab – oh! Appeal for hand ball! Not given. There's an arching pass up front to find Yockenthwaite...*can* it find Yockenthwaite? Where *is* Yockenthwaite?'

Yockenthwaite missed the ball because he was deep in some long grass searching for a three-leafed clover, so it went straight to Kettlewell. The Rottentrolls' garlic pasty maestro kicked the ball high into the air, and when it came down it found...

'Penyghent!' screamed Commander Harris. 'That was Penyghent with a *superb* header! There was me assuming she'd be in goal, but this young girl has set the valley alight!'

By half time Penyghent had scored with two volleys and a scorching thirty-foot drive. Far from being the girlie stuck in goal, she was

turning out to be a star player who ran like lightning and was harder to mark than an 'A' Level physics exam paper. It was during the half time break that Blacksyke sidled over to the players with a tray of glasses filled with a blue liquid...

'Refreshments!' she called out. 'Get yer refreshments here!'

'What's this?' asked Yockenthwaite, pointing at a glass.

'It's me new blueberry-flavoured Aerobitronic Sports Liquid,' said Blacksyke from behind her veil.

'Well that's very kind of you to offer,' said Askrigg, reaching for a glass.

'It's 50p a glass,' said Blacksyke, moving the tray out of reach.

'50p?' said Great Nab. 'That's an obscene mark-up, man!'

'Yeah, like totally spurious pricing,' agreed Small Nab. 'I'll just have water.'

So nobody accepted Blacksyke's Aerobitronic Sports Liquid and during the second half Penyghent went on to score two more goals. She ended the game being generally accepted as the best player in the whole of Troller's Ghyll.

'I can't believe it!' panted Roger. 'Y'r better than me!'

'Ta,' said Penyghent.

'I didn't think girls could play football,' said Yockenthwaite.

And the next day, when everyone decided it would be a great idea to have another game, a fight broke out over whose team she was going to be on. Which was all very nice for Penyghent, who soon realised she was onto a good thing and could ask for lots of favours...

'I'll be on the team...' she said, making a big production out of thinking hard, '...that has the best oranges.'

'That's us!' shouted Aysgarth excitedly. 'We've got *lovely* oranges on our team, Penyghent!'

'No way, man!' butted in Great Nab. '*Our* oranges are radically better!'

Soon Penyghent was being treated like a real star. She had her own private changing room and as much fruit as she could eat, if not more. Which was when Blacksyke came a-knocking on her door...

'Hello dearie...'

'What d'you want Blacksyke?' asked Penyghent dismissively. 'I've got to go out in a minute and win a football match quite superbly.'

'Just a little word, dearie,' smiled Blacksyke, 'about sponsorship.'

'Sponsorship?' said Penyghent. 'What's that?'

'Oh it's a *marvellous* thing, dearie,' said Blacksyke, making herself comfortable. 'What happens is...I've got something I want people to buy...'

'Your horrible, foul-tasting gunky old drink?' interrupted Penyghent.

'My blueberry-flavoured *Aerobitronic* Sports Liquid, dearie,' said Blacksyke sternly. 'And people *will* buy it if they think someone they admire drinks it...a big sports star, for example. Like you.'

'Drink it?' sneered Penyghent. 'It's rubbish – '*Aerobitronic*' is a load of guff, it doesn't mean anything, I looked it up in a dictionary! Plus, it smells horrible. Why on earth would I say I drink it?'

'Because...' Blacksyke whispered in Penyghent's ear, 'I'll give you *lots* of money if you do.'

And the next thing anyone knew, Penyghent was starring in a very expensive advert on RTV which showed her scoring goal after fantastic goal, her long hair flying behind her and the ball slamming into the back of the net in gorgeous slow-motion. Then, in softly-lit close-up, she turned to the camera and said: 'Hi, I'm

Penyghent. You know, a lot of people have asked what makes me such a fantastic footballer – is it training? Dedication? No. It's (holds up bottle) *Blacksyke's blueberry-flavoured Aerobitronic Sports Liquid!* It keeps me the top footballer in the valley...it could do the same for you! Buy loads!'

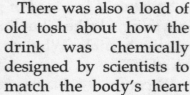

There was also a load of old tosh about how the drink was chemically designed by scientists to match the body's heart rate, and the ad was on all the time. And there were posters – did I mention the posters?

Anyway, it worked, because no sooner had the campaign started than Blacksyke got a visitor...

'Well, well, well,' she said as she opened the door to her cave late one night, 'who have we here? Can it be the first customer wanting to buy some of my Aerobitronic Sports Liquid?'

'Weeee!!' said Little Strid, holding up her piggy bank.

Uh-oh...someone had obviously been watching TV well past their bedtime and had crawled out of their cot...

'Let's see if you've got enough money,' said Blacksyke, smashing the piggy bank on a rock.

'Weeeee – Penyghent!' shrilled poor Little Strid excitedly.

'You want to be like Penyghent, do you, you little sprog?' asked Blacksyke, taking the money and handing over a can. 'Well *this* is the drink that'll do it – *HAHAHAHAHAHA!!*'

As it happens, the Aerobitronic Sports Liquid didn't make Little Strid like Penyghent at all...in fact it made her go all woozy, feel like nothing on Earth and lie in her cot looking awful. And it made Kettlewell, her mum, go into a flat panic.

'WAA-AAH! I don't know what's the matter,' she wailed, clinging to Aysgarth, 'I found her like this when I came to wake her up.'

'Poor little thing,' said Aysgarth. 'What d'you think might be wrong with her, Penyghent?'

'I don't know, I just d...' suddenly Penyghent spotted the empty can of Aerobitronic Sports Liquid in the corner of the room. Her heart almost stopped. 'Oh no...'

'Do you know what?' said Kettlewell. 'I saw an advertisement for that new aerobi-whatsit sports drink on TV last night – I bet that'd help my Little Strid!'

'It's supposed to be really good stuff, that is,' nodded Yockenthwaite.

'Pardon?' said Penyghent.

'Right...like they said, it's chemically rated to design your heart...or something,' nodded Aysgarth. 'That might make her feel fit again!'

'I'll go and buy some now!' said Kettlewell, picking up her baby and rushing out of the cave, followed by Aysgarth, Yockenthwaite and a very worried Penyghent.

'Hold on!' said Penyghent, as Kettlewell knocked on Blacksyke's door. 'I'm not sure you should give her any of that stuff...'

'Don't be daft!' said Yockenthwaite. '*You*

drink it and look how fit you are!'

'No, but...'

'You said in the advert it makes you feel fit and healthy,' added Yockenthwaite.

'Ah – more customers!' said Blacksyke, opening her door, taking Kettlewell's money and handing over a can. 'Thank you.'

Penyghent was beside herself. What could she do? She knew the Aerobitronic Sports Liquid had made Little Strid ill in the first place, and here the poor thing was, about to be dosed up with loads and loads more of the stuff. Tons of it. Great barrel-loads...

'Stop!' Penyghent cried out, everyone turning to look at her. 'I've never drunk it...I've *never* drunk it *ever!* Blacksyke just paid me to say I had...*I* don't know where it comes from, or what's in it, and I shouldn't have done the advert but I was greedy and I wanted the money!'

And she burst out crying...at which point everyone turned to look at Blacksyke...

'Just what is in this drink?' asked Aysgarth.

'There's, ooh, strawberries, and sugar and fairies' tears,' said Blacksyke, counting the "ingredients" off on her fingers, 'and magic twinkly spring water from the...'

'BLACKSYKE!' shouted Aysgarth sternly.

'Puddles,' said Blacksyke.

'You let her baby drink *puddles!*'

'I'll deck yer!' screamed Kettlewell.

'No, Kettlewell!' said Aysgarth, standing between the chef and the cringing target of her anger. 'I think there's a *much* better punishment for two people who need to be taught a lesson. In a minute, two people are going to drink a can of this *lovely*, healthy drink to see how *they* like their own medicine!'

And so it was that the next day everyone met at the Valley Ground for another game of five-a-side...

'Is Penyghent not playing today?' asked Roger.

'No, she's er...happier staying somewhere near a sink, actually, King Roger,' said Aysgarth.

'What're we gonna do? We'll be one person short,' said Roger.

'No problem, we've sorted it out,' said Aysgarth, pointing to Little Strid sitting in her pram and heading balls like there was no tomorrow. 'Funnily enough there's an up-and-coming footballer in the valley who's feeling just fine!'

PART 7 (The Rottentroll Election Special)

The one thing England's always had a lot of is rain. Let's face it, if rain were worth a lot of dosh, we'd all be rolling in it – and by that I mean money, not puddles. One of the places that seems to get more than its fair share of the wet stuff is Troller's Ghyll. When it rains in Troller's Ghyll it does it with gusto, let me tell you.

First, all the dust turns to mud, the trees turn into, well...wet trees...and Rottentrolls turn into bored Rottentrolls who can't go out because it's raining. And a bored Rottentroll could win First Prize in the World *I'm the Most Bored Person on Earth* competition, no trouble at all.

'I'm bored,' said Yockenthwaite on one wet day. 'Bored, bored, bored.'

'Don't be so *boring!*' yelled Kettlewell, the dangerous chef.

'I know!' said Penyghent brightly. 'Why don't we have a drawing competition?'

She was sitting between Yockenthwaite and Kettlewell in a cave entrance, and they both turned and looked at her as if she'd suggested swimming with piranhas.

'No, no, no!' said Kettlewell firmly. 'I think we

should have an arm wrestling contest, I do.'

'Tell y'what,' beamed Yockenthwaite, 'why don't we have a massive chariot race round the cave, with huge teams of beautiful white horses?'

Now it was his turn to be stared at.

'That's just a daft idea, in't it?' whispered Yockenthwaite.

Well of course it was a daft idea. It's a well known fact in Troller's Ghyll that Yockenthwaite's best thing is daft ideas...in fact it's his *only* thing. The problem was, when it rained King Roger never came to the valley (not being a big fan of soggy saddles, soaked trainers and stupid-looking kagouls...and who can blame him?) and when King Roger didn't come to the valley no one could make their mind up about anything at all. Bit pathetic, really, but that's Rottentrolls for you.

Anyway, 24 hours later, the sun was shining, the sky was blue and there was a light breeze. Perfect cycling weather, and so who should turn up in the valley but Roger, King of the Rottentrolls...

'There was no one to make a decision y'see, King Roger,' said Penyghent as she walked along with him, explaining what a boring day everyone had had. 'There was, like, no one in charge, so we didn't do anything.'

'I see,' said Roger, rubbing his hands and smiling. 'Well that's easy to sort out...I'll call a meeting...'

Roger liked calling meetings. It meant he could sit in the Great Cave on his throne (actually, it was an old dressing table, but to the Rottentrolls it was a throne) and tell people what to do.

'In the world outside Troller's Ghyll,' said Roger, 'as well as Kings and Queens, we have these things called 'Prime Ministers'.'

Yockenthwaite's hand shot up. 'I know them! I know them!' he said. 'Are they very small, round cheesy crackers?'

'No,' sighed Roger.

'Berk,' growled Aysgarth, throwing his pipe at Yockenthwaite.

'Prime Ministers,' Roger went on, after Aysgarth had got his pipe back, 'make decisions on who does what. You just need a Prime Minister to make decisions when I'm not here.'

'Well that's easy,' said Penyghent, pointing at Aysgarth, 'it'll be Dad. So let's...'

'Not necessarily,' boomed a deep, dark, cold, spine-shivering voice that came from the deep, dark, cold shadows and echoed, spine-shiveringly round the Great Cave. It was Blacksyke, the rottenest of the Rottentrolls.

'What if someone thinks they'd make a better job of being Prime Minister?' she asked. 'What if someone else wants a go? What happens then, King Roger?'

Everyone in the cave turned and looked at Roger.

'Well,' said Roger, his brain stalling in first gear as he tried to think what did happen under these circumstances. Everyone nodded, waiting in anticipation for his words of wisdom.

'In the world outside Troller's Ghyll,' he said, suddenly remembering, 'we have an election!'

And so it was that the first Rottentroll General Election campaign began, between Aysgarth ('Vote for me, you know it makes sense!'), Blacksyke ('Vote for me, or else!') and Sigsworthy Crags ('Ar-ooooo!!'). Nobody took the slightest notice of Sigsworthy Crags because they all knew he was completely mad, so that left the two main contenders. Now Roger wasn't completely sure what happened during a General Election, as he'd only ever seen bits on the news, but he was pretty sure he knew how they started.

'OK, the first thing we do is have a debate,' said Roger, who was sitting at one end of the Great Table, the three candidates behind him. He was looking at the assembled audience of

Rottentrolls and trying to imagine that he was actually hosting a live TV show. Except that he was sitting under a sign on the wall which read *'WHO IS NICEST?'*

'And could we start the proceedings with a question from the floor, please?' he continued.

'Yeah, right,' said Great Nab, standing up. 'Name the lead singer in Oasis.'

Aysgarth looked at Blacksyke, nodding as if to say he thought it only right that ladies should go first; Blacksyke ignored the offer and shrugged. 'Who?' she said.

'Not *that* kind of question!' frowned Roger.

'Is it Shirley Bassey?' asked Sigsworthy Crags.

'Who?' said Great and Small Nab at the same time.

'Look, I mean *other* kinds of questions!' said Roger, waving his hands, trying to give the impression of, well, something else.

'I've never heard of Shirley Bassey,' Great Nab said to Small Nab.

'She must be well radical if *we've* never heard of her,' Small Nab raised his eyebrows at the thought of anyone that radical.

'Check out the music head on Sigsy!' grinned Great Nab.

'Vote for Sigsworthy!' yelled Small Nab, bouncing up and down excitedly.

'SHUT *UP!!*' yelled Roger, who realised he had to get the debate back on track before it simply became a good old shouting match which, when you think about it, is just like a proper General Election, really. 'Let's have a decent question. Yes, Penyghent?'

'Which of these two words best describes you?' Penyghent asked the three candidates. 'Is it 'nice', or 'horrid'?'

'Nice,' replied Aysgarth.

'Horrid,' glowered Blacksyke.

'Chocolate, with a smashing orangey bit in the middle,' said Sigsworthy. 'Ar-ooo!'

'Did you hear that?' said Penyghent, pointing at Blacksyke triumphantly. 'She admits she's horrid! It's all over!'

'Now listen up, dearie,' rumbled Blacksyke, her eyes almost burning holes in her black veil, 'just because someone says they're nice doesn't necessarily mean they are. Perhaps I'm being the most honest one here...admitting that I'm horrid.'

'Don't be ridiculous! Everyone knows my Dad's the most honest, upstanding troll in the Ghyll!'

'Really?' said Blacksyke. 'Well I think you'd better take a good look at the headline in tomorrow's newspaper, dearie...'

The next morning the first edition of the *Troller's Ghyll Daily Thing* came out with just one story on its front cover. The massive headline read: AYSGARTH KICKS SHEEP! and underneath it was a huge picture of a man, with a cut-out photo of Aysgarth's head rather amateurishly stuck on his shoulders, doing exactly that.

'That's not me in that photo!' said Aysgarth. 'Anyone with half a brain can see it's someone else's body with my head stuck on it!'

'Fooled me,' said Yockenthwaite.

'Don't worry, Dad,' said Penyghent. 'Everyone'll know it's rubbish.'

Oh will they, Penyghent...?

'Morning Commander Harris, I've come for my lesson in the ancient martial art of Jimjam YaHa.'

'Roger, King Roger, come in and sit...' said the Commander, who was reading the sports page of the *Daily Thing* and had just turned to look at the headlines. 'Hold on a toyty – "Aysgarth Kicks Sheep"?'

'Never,' said Roger, taking the paper. 'That's never true!'

'Well you know what they say,' the Commander nodded wisely, 'there's no smoke without fire.'

'What about when you've got a pile of damp leaves?' said Yockenthwaite.

And you have to admit, he had a point, about gardening at least. But he'd forgotten all about what we narrators like to call the 'Chinese Whisper Effect', which is what happens when a person at one end of, say the Great Table, tells the person sitting next to them that...

'Actually I *did* see Aysgrath standing near a sheep once, Small Nab.'

And that person tells the person next to them more, or less, the same thing...

'My little bro, he saw Aysgarth with a load of sheep, Kettlewell.'

But there's a little twist that means *they* then tell the person sitting next to them that...

'Great Nab saw Aysgarth in a load of sheep, sort of *nudging* them!'

And each time the story gets told it gets wronger and wronger until it's gone almost the whole way round the table and Trucklecrag (the disappointing magician) tells Askrigg...

'Asygarth singled out one particular sheep and gave it a push.'

So by the time Yockenthwaite tells Aysgarth what he's heard, it goes something like this...

'Apparently, on the 23rd of this month, you took a fifty metre run-up down the valley, jumped in the air shouting 'I am Eric Cantona!' and kicked this sheep right up the bottom.'
     '*What?*' squealed Penyghent.
     'Who's Eric Cantona?' said Asygarth.
     'That's a *terrible* lie!' Penyghent said, stamping her foot. 'We need to publicly deny it.'

Next morning there was a small, bright orange card nailed to a fence post, which read:
AYSGARTH HEREBY DENIES HE HAS *EVER* KICKED A SHEEP. *Signed* Aysgarth.

'That should do the trick,' said Penyghent, putting a hammer away in her back pocket. 'That orange makes it quite eye-catching, don't you think, Yockenthwaite?'

'Er, not bad,' said Yockenthwaite. 'But have you seen what's round the corner?'

Round the corner was a billboard the size of a tennis court. On it was a gigantic photo of Aysgarth with his real eyes replaced by evil red ones, and the words:

SAME OLD AYSGARTH
SAME OLD SHEEP-KICKER

'Right!' snarled Penyghent. 'I've had just about enough of this!' she snarled in an even snarlier way, and stormed off to the Great Cave, where she found Blacksyke innocently doing some knitting.

'That does it, you horrid old bag!'

'Stop it, Penyghent!' said Aysgarth. But there was no stopping her.

'My Dad does *not* kick sheep!' she snarled (again). 'If anyone round here kicks sheep it's you, you nasty old bat!'

'Sorry dear, I really can't talk at the moment,' simpered Blacksyke, her needles clicking like a full set of false teeth. 'I'm busy knitting these toilet roll covers for homeless people.'

'That's nice of her, in't it,' said Great Nab.

Penyghent turned on the crowd. 'Nice? NICE?!' she yelled. 'What do homeless people want with *toilet roll covers?* She's just doing pointless things to trick you into *thinking* she's nice – can't you see?'

But, as is the way with these things, the time for campaigning, kissing babies and making lots of promises you're never, ever going to keep was over all too quickly and it was suddenly...Election Day!

All the Rottentrolls had got up very early and gathered in the Great Cave, where someone had let Trucklecrag take charge of things.

'Rottentrolls and trollslips,' he beamed. 'We are now ready to vote in the first Rottentroll General Election!'
Everyone went *'Ooooooh!!'*
'Here you can see the fantastic vote-counting machine I've magicked up!'
Everyone went *'Ahhhhhh!'* as they looked at the wooden frame holding two metal buckets, various elastic bands and a tangle of pipes.
'Now listen carefully,' Trucklecrag went on. 'To vote for Aysgarth, put a cup of water into a tin on this rotating elastic band...to vote for Blacksyke, put a cup in t'other one.'
Everyone went *'Ummmm...'*

'The water is then con-ducted, like, down these cunningly con-structed pipes.' Trucklecrag pointed to the pipes, just in case anyone was unaware what they were, 'Then it will be drunk by one or other of the Nab Twins!'

Everyone looked at the Nab Twins.

'At the end of the voting procedure we wait until one of the Nab Twins has to go to t'toilet,' said Trucklecrag. 'Now, the winner will be the person – Aysgarth or, like, Blacksyke – whose Nab Twin goes to the toilet *last*. Or first. Or...er...'

'Couldn't we just stick our hands up?' asked Penyghent.

'Or y'could do it that way,' nodded Trucklecrag. Just then Roger burst into the cave, all in a muck sweat and panting like a dog left in the car on a hot day.

'Stop! Hold on!' he sputtered. 'Before you vote, I've just remembered – I forgot the most important thing of all! The debates and the posters are the frilly bits...the most important thing is your *policy!*'

'I know that!' said Yockenthwaite, putting his hand up. 'Isn't that the promise of what you're going to do if you get elected?'

'No...it's a small cheesy...' Roger stopped. 'No, you're right, yes. It's what Yockenthwaite said. Aysgarth – what's *your* policy?'

'Go on, Dad,' whispered Penyghent. 'Make something up...anything that's better than what Blacksyke'll say. Promise you'll do *anything* – make it up!'

'I can't do that, Penyghent,' said Aysgarth, standing up to speak. 'Fellow Rottentrolls, I'm not going to promise you anything as your Prime Minister...except that I'll *try* to build into your lives a little more happiness, and a little more peace. Thank you.'

All the Rottentrolls nodded to each other and Roger gave Penyghent a quietly confident thumbs-up.

'And now, Blacksyke?' said Roger.

'I promise to build you all a Leisure Centre!' said Blacksyke, standing up and activating a mechanism that:

1 – Unfurled a banner that read 'ROTTENTROLL LEISURE CENTRE'.

2 – Started music playing.

3 – Revealed a scale model showing tennis courts; a swimming pool; flood-lit, dome-style ping pong facilities; a sports hall; other stuff...oooh, yes, and a spiffy new gym.

To a man (and a woman, and a child) all the Rottentrolls threw their hats (and Yockenthwaite) in the air, cheered and elected Blacksyke by an overwhelming majority. Which only goes to show that you can take a horse to water, but you can't make it think...or something. It definitely shows something, anyway.

The very next day a big sign, with a rather nice illustration of the leisure centre, got put up. On it were the words: COMPLETION DATE – NEXT WEEK.

'Yo-o!' said Yockenthwaite. 'I can't wait to have a swim in the new pool!'

'You don't *swim* in swimming pools, man!' sneered Great Nab.

'No!' agreed Small Nab. 'You run along the side, jump off the springboard flapping your arms shouting "Superchicken!!"...and then get chucked out!'

'*Swim!*' said Great Nab.

'Wuss,' said Small Nab.

'Whatever,' smiled Yockenthwaite, to whom insults were a part of normal conversation. 'Let's go and ask Blacksyke when it'll be ready'.

Now you've probably never seen Blacksyke's cave before. It's not a place people visit very much because it's cold and damp, with a door made out of disgusting old rags, and, well, Blacksyke lives there.

But when Yockenthwaite and the Nab Twins

arrived at the front door they found the rags replaced by a shiny new black affair with a polished brass number on it. The number 10. And there were iron railings either side of it too.

'Shall I knock?' asked Yockenthwaite, and then did without waiting for a reply.

'Ent-*eeer!*' said a muffled voice.

'Woww-w!' Yockenthwaite walked in and looked round at the bookcases full of leatherbound books, the computer screens, a ginormous picture window that overlooked the valley and a desk the size of a ping pong table. Behind it sat Blacksyke, in a swishy leather swivel chair. Nice.

'Totally outrageous office furniture, man!' said Great Nab.

'What d'you want?' growled Blacksyke.

'Er, we were wondering when the swimming pool's going to be ready.'

'The *swimming* pool?' said Blacksyke, dismissively. 'I've only just built myself an office. You don't expect me to build a swimming pool till I've sorted myself out a private jacuzzi, do you?'

'Er, 'spose not...obviously,' said Yockenthwaite, wondering what on earth a jacuzzi was. 'But when..?'

'Soon, soon,' Blacksyke turned the chair round to look out of the window. 'Read my lips – S-O-O-N...'

'SOON' turned out to be a slight exaggeration, and the words 'NEXT WEEK' on the big sign were changed to 'IN A BIT'. And when Askrigg and Penyghent went to ask Blacksyke when the new outdoor, flood-lit ping pong dome would be ready, they found her in her new jacuzzi. All she would say was that the dome couldn't be started until her sun patio was finished.

While all this was going on, or rather, while the new Leisure Centre *wasn't* going on, King Roger was down in the Ghyll busily trying to learn the ancient martial art of Jimjam YaHa with Commander Harris...

'Jimjam-YaHa!' Roger, standing in his new Jimjam-YaHa beginners T-shirt, with his arms outstretched, looked at the Commander.

'Not bad,' said the Commander, 'not bad at all...but, tragically, your little finger moved at the final moment; so, instead of knocking some bloke off his bike over the moor, you've in fact tickled a chap in the ribs somewhere in Cheltenham.'

As the days went on, the information on the Leisure Centre sign changed until it read: COMPLETION DATE – OCTEMBER 36th, which made perfect sense to Yockenthwaite, if no one else.

And when someone went to Blacksyke's cave

to ask about the new gymnasium, they found Blacksyke on her new sun patio, sipping a cocktail.

'Gymnasium!' she said. 'You don't expect me to build a gym*nasium* before I've built myself a Scandanavian sauna, do you?'

And when someone asked Blacksyke about the sports hall they found her in a small steam-filled wooded room, and she said:

'You don't expect me to build a sports hall till I've completed me 90-metre ski-jump, do you?'

And then, when someone enquired if the new Prime Minister had any idea when the snooker room might be ready, she replied (while on skis):

'You don't *really* expect me to do a snooker room till I've had me swimming pool filled with Iced Gems – with the biscuity parts bitten off – do you?'

Finally, enough was enough...

'Blacksyke!' said Penyghent, slamming the door to the Prime Minister's cave open and striding in. 'You *promised* us a Leisure Centre!'
  'No I didn't,' replied Blacksyke. 'What I said

was er, er 'cheese'...I promised you some small cheesy crackers.'

'YOU DID NOT!' roared Penyghent. 'AND WE DEMAND A PUBLIC STATEMENT!!'

So, not long afterwards, Blacksyke emerged from Number 10 to stand in front of loads of microphones that weren't actually plugged into anything, and weren't needed because everyone was only a few feet away.

'Rottentrolls,' she said. 'We stand here before you today to say that when we made the promise of a certain Leisure Centre, there were certain outstanding building commitments of which, at the time, we were unaware.'

'Fibber!' hissed Penyghent.

'Double-dealer!' muttered Kettlewell.

'Leisure Centre promiser, and then not builder-er!' said Yockenthwaite.

'Start building now, Blacksyke!' Penyghent handed the PM a spade.

'Can't dig.'

'Give us the plans and *we'll* dig,' said Penyghent.

'Haven't got any.'

'Give us the number of a builder then,' demanded Penyghent.

'Haven't got a *Yellow Pages*.'

'Hold on a minute,' said Yockenthwaite, as

a terrible truth began to dawn on each and every Rottentroll. 'Doesn't being elected *make* you keep your promises?'

'No – *Ha-hahahaha!!*' shrieked Blacksyke. 'And it's too late now cos I'm elected and I'm gonna be here for five years...five long, dark, *terrible* years – *A-hahahahahaha!!*'

And this was when King Roger walked in, wondering what all the manic laughter and shouting was all about.

'What's the matter?' he asked.

The assembled Rottentrolls all looked at each other in a silence so quiet you could have heard a pin drop. A tiny pin. On a *very* thick carpet. Interestingly, it was this silence which meant they all heard the strange gurgling sound. After waiting for a couple of minutes to make sure it wasn't Yockenthwaite's stomach, everyone followed the noise to an old, disused cave at the valley top and pushed Yockenthwaite in to see what it was...

'Yo-o...' he said, very quietly.

'It's beautiful,' whispered Penyghent, who'd come in after him.

'Totally radical indoor gardening experience, man,' said an awestruck Great Nab.

'Has this always been here?' asked Roger.

'No,' said Aysgarth, who was sitting on a bench smoking his pipe. 'I built it.'

'Aysgarth?' frowned Kettlewell. 'How did you grow all these flowers in a cave?'

'I didn't,' said Aysgrath. 'They're all dried

flowers, and I made the trees...the grass is all cut-up straw painted green...and the waterfall is all rainwater I diverted through a gully.'

'But, Dad...why?' asked Penyghent.

'Well...I promised I'd try to build a little more happiness and a little more peace, didn't I?' Aysgarth explained. 'This whole election thing started because none of us could decide what to do when it was raining...so I built this sort of little indoor valley.'

'But, like, y'didn't have to actually *do* it, man,' said Great Nab.

'Right,' agreed Small Nab, 'because, like, y'were pretty squarely *not* elected.'

'Doesn't matter, boys,' said Aysgarth. 'No point in making a promise if y'don't intend to keep it, is there?'

'Er, King Roger?' Yockenthwaite tugged on Roger's cardigan to get his attention. 'What happens if everyone suddenly realises that they've elected the wrong person?'

'Well...the grown-up thing to do is have another election,' said Roger.

'And what's the *not* grown-up thing to do?' enquired Yockenthwaite.

Which is how the first Rottentroll revolution began.

Everyone (except Blacksyke, of course) went out and got tatty red flags, banners which read

'NICK OFF!' and 'GET OUT YOU OLD BAT' and torches – by which I mean the ones you set fire to, not ones with batteries – and stormed Blacksyke's cave.

'Blacksyke!' yelled Roger, steam-rollering the front door down. 'The Rottentrolls don't want you as their Prime Minister any more!'

'Well tough bun cookie!' screeched Blacksyke. 'They've got me – *ah-hahahahaha!!!*'

'I'm going to ask you, politely, to give up your office,' said Roger, politely.

'NEVER!' screamed Blacksyke, heaving a desk-tidy in Roger's general direction. 'GET OUT!'

'Blacksyke,' grimaced Roger, as the desk-tidy hit him, 'I don't want to have to use force...'

'You haven't got the power to force me to do anything,' cackled Blacksyke, chucking a cocktail glass his way, 'you PLEB!'

'Watch it, Blacksyke!' warned Roger, waving a finger at her. 'I've got the power to make that bookcase over there flatten you so's you'll have to be *carried* out of here!'

'Rubbish!' replied Blacksyke. 'There's no way you could move something it took a fork-lift truck to get in here!'

'Really? Watch me...' said Roger, pointing at the bookcase and summoning up all his training. 'Jimjam YaHa!'

Tragically, Roger wasn't very good at Jimjam YaHa yet, so instead of flattening Blacksyke, one book on the bookcase sort of flopped down on its side.

'A-*hahahaha!!* Pathetic!' squealed Blacksyke. 'Get out of here, you with your stupid Jimjam YaHa!'

Tragically, for Blacksyke, it turned out that she was, without knowing it, completely brilliant at Jimjam YaHa. On her words, the bookcase leapt across the room and slammed into her and her ping pong table-sized desk. Quite impressive, actually.

And so it was that Aysgarth came to be elected as the new Prime Minister, Blacksyke got given the job of cleaning the indoor valley – to teach her all about keeping promises – and everyone got to have a go in the jacuzzi.

'Wild feeling, man!' said Great Nab. 'It's like a bath with loads of bubbles coming up from the bottom!'

'You know,' pondered Yockenthwaite, 'I'm sure I've had this feeling before.'

'I don't want to hear about it, thank you very much,' said Penyghent.

PART 8 (The Complimentary Cafetiere)

As you know by now, Yockenthwaite is the most stupid of the Rottentrolls. In fact, if you put a stick in the ground and arranged all the Rottentrolls at distances from it appropriate to how stupid they were, Penyghent, the cleverest, would be standing right by the stick. All the rest of the Rottentrolls would be somewhere in the valley and Yockenthwaite...well, Yockenthwaite would be in a small village outside Poona in western India.

In reality (if you can use that word to describe Troller's Ghyll), Yockenthwaite was out for a walk one morning when he found a leaflet that had blown into the secret valley...

'What's this then?' he said, picking it up. '"THE CARPET VALET DELUXE – it's much more than just a vacuum cleaner! Send for a FREE demonstration and receive your complimentary cafetiere!'...wow!'

If there had been such a thing as a not-stupid Yockenthwaite he would have said 'What I *definitely* shouldn't do now is send this leaflet off, because I don't have any carpets, I don't know what a cafetiere is, and we mustn't *ever* let any humans into the valley.'

But, of course, Yockenthwaite *was* completely stupid.

'Yo-o!' he grinned to himself, as he walked back from the post box. 'A cafetiere – beezer, wait till I tell the others!'

'You did *what?*' exploded Roger, on hearing Yockenthwaite's news.

'But we haven't *got* any carpets!' said Penyghent.

'But y'get a free cafetiere!' said Yockenthwaite.

'Y'don't even know what one is, man,' sneered Great Nab.

'I do, I do!' replied Yockenthwaite. 'I'm *fairly* sure it's a kind of tea shop that's built on more than one level...'

'No it's not,' sighed Roger, 'it's a small glass jug you make coffee in.'

'Right,' nodded Yockenthwaite. 'That's not as good, then, is it?'

'No. And most of all – most *seriously* of all,' said Aysgarth, 'we must never *ever* allow any humans to enter the valley!'

'But we let King Roger in!' Yockenthwaite pointed out.

'I'm your *King!* I care about you, you great berk!' said Roger. 'Any other human finding a load of Trolls here would...would put you in a *circus!* Put you on *day*time TV! There'll be a theme park! Any other human coming in here could change this valley for*ever*, and, thanks to *your* invitation, there's probably one heading this way right now!'

And indeed there was. His name was Ian Clucas, he drove a ten-year-old red Sierra estate (with one of those green cardboard trees hanging from the rear-view mirror) and he was in hyper-sales mode. He really *wanted* to sell a vacuum cleaner today, because it was a GREAT vacuum cleaner, and because he was a GREAT vacuum cleaner salesman, and he *wanted* this sale...he was a dog, the sale was a rabbit and he was going to *grab* it...

'What's that?' muttered Commander Harris,

spotting a blip on his early-warning radar scanner. 'Looks suspiciously like a motor ve-hicle to me...better get on the tannoy!'

Swinging round in his chair, the Commander grabbed a microphone, flicked a switch and began broadcasting his message of doom to the Rottentrolls. *'Incoming! Incoming!'* he yelled. 'Unidentified ve-hicle approaching!'

This somewhat hysterical announcement was followed by some truly hysterical behaviour. You couldn't see for panicking Rottentrolls running hither, and, naturally, thither, with their arms waving about as they wailed, prayed and set about writing their Last Will and Testaments.

'STOP! CALM DOWN! IT'S OK!' yelled Roger (it has to be said, hysterically). 'I know what to do – my Mum and Step-dad had a salesman round once, and all you have to do is listen to what they say, tell 'em "no thanks" and they go!'

'But we can't let a human see us!' wailed Aysgarth. 'We're doomed!'

Cue a re-run of the previously described hysterical behaviour. At which point Roger yelled:

'Don't start *that* again. I'll handle this, just get out of sight and *keep* out of sight!'

And so it was that when Ian the salesman came into the valley, carrying his briefcase and demonstration vacuum cleaner and muttering something about how he was a cat and the sale was a mouse, he was met by a single, quite friendly-looking, boy...

'Hello,' said Roger.

'Ah...hello, yes...I'm looking for a...' Ian got out a clipboard from his briefcase and checked it, '...for a Mr Y Ockenthwaite!'

'Yes...' said Roger, his fingers crossed behind his back, 'that's me.'

'OK...fine...great!' said Ian, desperately trying to remember why the word 'FISHDUNK' had suddenly popped into his head. And then it came to him...the letter F stood for 'First Impressions'... 'Right – hi, my name's Ian! D'you know, I was nearly late for our appointment because I was staring at my carpets! I see you're asking yourself "Why was Ian staring at his carpets?" and the answer is, because I've got a *Carpet Valet Deluxe* and so my carpets surprise me every time I look at them!'

Roger didn't say anything.

'Right,' said Ian, remembering the letter I stood for 'If', as in...'If you're going to say something, sir, don't – just look at how small the nozzle on this model is! How big is the nozzle on your current vacuum cleaner?'

Roger stayed as silent as a cup of tea. He knew he just had to wait, say 'no' and the salesman would go away.

'Bigger than this, I'll bet – *this* is the smallest nozzle on *any* vacuum cleaner in the world!' grinned Ian, who had come to the letter S, which stood for 'Surprise him'... 'Now I know you're thinking "Three thousand pounds is a lot to spend on a vacuum cleaner", but let me tell you, this isn't *just* a vacuum cleaner...it's a

Home Cleaning System. It'll clean your curtains, it'll clean your pets, it'll clean all your windows! With a special attachment it'll blow-dry your hair and inflate rubber paddling pools! This is so much *more* than a vacuum cleaner, Mr Ockenthwaite – so much more, this is...'

Now at this point two things happened to Ian; firstly, he ran out of breath, and secondly he realised exactly where he was and who he was talking to...

'...this is the middle of nowhere and you are a child. And you sent the form back to play a trick on me. And I fell for it because I'm desperate to sell a vacuum cleaner!' Ian bent down to look Roger straight in the eye. 'I'm desperate because I got made redundant from the building society 18 months ago and no one will employ a 55-year old. I'm so...*so* desperate to sell my first one of these *stupid* vacuum cleaners...'

Ian threw the nozzle down in disgust, and collapsed on a rock with his head in his hands. Sobbing. Quietly. Roger was quite used to this because the supply teachers at his school did it all the time.

'Look mister...' he said.
    'Any news on the cafetiere?' whispered

Yockenthwaite, bobbing up from behind a bush.

'Look, Mr Salesman...' Roger went on, waving Yockenthwaite back down.

'Salesman?' said Ian, blowing his nose. 'I'm not a salesman, I'm a *fails*man!'

'I'm sure it's a lovely vacuum cleaner,' said Roger.

'It's not. It's *rubbish*,' said Ian. 'It's £3,000! It'd be cheaper to move house every time it needed dusting!'

'Well...it cleans pets,' offered Roger.

'Only of they're the size of a moose,' said Ian. 'If they're any smaller it just sucks them up...'

'OK, well it's compact,' said Roger, who was beginning to run out of positive things to say about something he didn't want.

'The nozzle is,' agreed Ian. 'But look at the size of the box it's attached to...'

Roger looked. He had to admit that it sort of defined the word 'big'. It was like a kennel on wheels, with a trunk...no, it was more like a small, black, square elephant. Or maybe it was like an incredibly large, boxy mouse, thought Roger...a large, boxy mouse with a half-inflated weather balloon-style dust bag for a bottom.

'Oh, Ian Clucas, what have you become?' wailed Ian Clucas, staring at the endless moor. 'I had dreams, you know. I had dreams about what I'd do with my life. Not only haven't I achieved any of them...I've even forgotten what they were!'

'Oh...' said Roger, who was wondering what to do next because supply teachers normally just ran out of the classroom crying, they didn't actually *talk* to you.

'Y'know what I need to do?' said Ian, 'I need to remember my dreams. Just spend time on my own, somewhere quiet like this valley...in fact that's what I'll do! I'll make a tent out of this rotten vacuum cleaner's great big dust bag and stay here until I get my life sorted out!'

Cue another bout of intense panic as the Rottentrolls lost it completely. Which, as you must have realised by now, is something they were all incredibly good at. Even Yockenthwaite, who wasn't good at anything except being stupid. Which is why they were all having to panic in the first place.

'STOP! CALM DOWN! *SHHHHH!*' hissed Roger as he presided over a meeting he'd called in the Great Cave. 'Right...I declare a State of Emergency! The salesman says he's staying in the valley, so there's going to be a total curfew – no Rottentroll must come out of their cave tonight...not a single one of you!'

As night fell, Roger went up to Commander Harris's command hut and sat with him as he kept track of Ian Clucas's movements on his radar screens...

'If you see him going towards a Rottentroll cave, Commander...' Roger whispered in his ear.

'Don't worry, King Roger,' said the Commander, 'it's all covered. If the target...'

'Salesman...'

'If the *salesman* strays into a danger zone, I'll give the sign,' said the Commander. 'Whereupon a crack squad of Silently Armed Sheep will move down from the upper field and create a disturbance – thus distracting him.'

'How long will that take?'

'About two hours, depending on how good the grass is on the way.'

'Well *that's* no use!'

'With respect Your Majesty,' sighed the Commander. 'Why don't you just lie in wait and Jimjam YaHa him?'

'Cos I haven't learned how to do it properly yet, have I?' said Roger. 'Not only am I *only* on the first level of Jimjam, I have to go home now cos it's getting late. If that salesman discovers the Rottentrolls it's all over...for ever. To be frank, Commander, I think all y'can do is sit here with your hooves crossed.'

'Roger, King Roger,' said the Commander. As Roger left the hut, he did indeed cross his hooves and fell slowly off his chair. 'Now I wonder why he suggested that...' he said as he hit the ground.

As King Roger left to go home, Ian the salesman settled down for the night in his makeshift dust bag tent and all the Rottentrolls did as they were told and stayed in their caves. Soon, the valley was asleep and dreaming...

Penyghent was dreaming about being the cleverest person in the world and scoring maximum points (no passes or wrong answers) on her Mastermind specialist subject of 'World History Since the Dawn of Time'. Trucklecrag was dreaming about being on TV and doing a magic trick that turned Paul Daniels into a small pile of sheep doo. And Yockenthwaite was dreaming about...a cafetiere.

It, by which I mean the brown box Yockenthwaite had to imagine because he still had no idea what a cafetiere looked like, talked gently to him, telling him how beautiful it was...

'My cafetiere!' squeaked Yockenthwaite, as his fabulous dream woke him up. 'I've *got* to see it just once. I'm sure King Roger won't mind if I break the curfew a little *tiny* bit.'

Sneaking out of his cave, Yockenthwaite crept

up to the place where Ian the salesman was camped, slowly and surely and just like a...well, just like a Rottentroll who knew very well he shouldn't be sneaking up to where Ian the salesman was camped.

'It must be in the tenty thing,' Yockenthwaite muttered. 'All I need is one little tiny, weeny, itsy bitsy, ever-so small little peep-y kind of...'

Walking on the tippiest of toes, Yockenthwaite edged towards the tenty thing. But as he reached to pull back the flap and creep inside, what he had failed to realise was that he wasn't out late at night any more...it was so late it had come all the way round and was nearly morning. *So* nearly morning, in fact, that as Yockenthwaite pulled the tent flap back, the sun came out from behind Rumble Rock.

Ian the salesman woke up as the sun shone right in his eyes, and he blinked. Yockenthwaite froze as he witnessed the sight of the first adult human ever to set eyes on a Rottentroll. He had no idea what to do, so he simply finished the sentence he'd already started.

'...look at the cafetiere.'

Then he turned and hared off down the valley.

'What's happened?' panted Roger, who'd raced back up to the valley without even having his usual bowl of Cocopops.

'W-*AAAAAAAHH!!*' sobbed Yockenthwaite.

'Tell me he didn't see anyone!' said Roger.

But before anyone could say anything, even about how thunderously stupid Yockenthwaite had been, they all heard the sound of someone laughing. Someone very like Ian the salesman.

'Everyone hide!' said Roger. 'I'll go out and see what he's got to say.'

'Hello, Mr Ockenthwaite!' grinned Ian, when he spotted Roger coming towards him. 'You'll *never* guess what's happened...what came to me in the night!'

'I've got a pretty good idea,' sighed Roger. 'Now listen...'

'I had a dream!' said Ian, with a grin like a melon slice.

'...the Rottentrolls...what did you say?'

'Last night I dreamt there was this light, in my eyes...a bright light,' explained Ian. 'And against it there was this silhouette of a figure, a strange little ugly goblin, saying "look at the cafetiere"!'

'I'll kill him!' muttered Roger.

'I'm sorry,' whispered Yockenthwaite from behind a nearby bush.

'And that was it!' continued Ian excitedly. 'My brain was obviously trying to remind me of the thing I always wanted to do! My dream was that I wanted to open a café!'

'A what?'

'A café...ever since I was your age, all I've ever wanted was to have a big, fantastic café,' said Ian. 'On more than one level.'

'So, in a sense, I was right about the...' whispered Yockenthwaite.

'*Shut it!*' hissed Roger.

'Forget the stupid vacuum cleaners – I'm going to open a café with tea buns and Eccles cakes!' said Ian, bringing a smallish glass jug with a metal plunger out from behind his back. 'And do you know what I'm going to do with this complimentary cafetiere?'

'Give it to me?' whispered the hiding Yockenthwaite.

'I'm going to put it in a glass case behind the till to remind me of the wonderful, wonderful day you played a trick and invited me up to this valley!' said Ian. 'Bye, bye!'

And with that, Ian Clucas – soon-to-be-café-owner – skipped happily out of the valley, never to be seen again. Except for when he stopped and turned for a second to ask...

'Back there...a few moments ago...what was it

you started saying? What's a Rottentroll?'

'It's, er...nothing,' replied Roger. 'It's just a legend. "Rottentrolls" were believed to be small, annoying creatures who never did as they were told – and as a result, had to spend hours collecting rubbish as a punishment.'

'OK!' said Ian, going off one way.

'I'll get a bin sack then, shall I?' said Yockenthwaite, going off the other.

And that was that. The day saved by one young chap from Hugh Gaitskell Crescent, Cowgill. The Rottentroll future secure, until the next time some idiot decided to reply to an advert for something he didn't want or need – plus the endless moor kept free of roaming hordes of salesmen, desperate to sell anything to anyone, particularly if they had a van-load of vacuum cleaners.

Which reminds me of a funny thought I had the other day...wouldn't it have been odd if the man who invented the vacuum cleaner had been called Mr Firth (for instance) instead of Mr Hoover. You'd go to a shop, buy a Firth, take it home and get on with the firthing! Oh well, it made me laugh...now, I suppose, I'd better get on with what we narrators call The Final Paragraph.

Uh-hum:

'And so it was that Troller's Ghyll remained a hidden, secret place of mad rocks and even madder trolls. Which was good, because the world already has enough rubbish on daytime TV, and needs another theme park like a hole in the head...'

There you are, that's it...THE END.